"G-goodbye!"

Another pause, as Chance scrutinized her face. Then he straightened and demanded, "Why?" He seemed so angry.

Mary's eyes rounded and then she looked down at her tangled fingers. "Oooh...I'm...sooo...busy." This was too hard. It was a fine, brave attempt, but she just couldn't come out and say that she'd heard he was a womanizer and a cheat.

"You're not that busy," he said in a low, clipped voice. "Why are you running away from me? You were just fine when I left you last night."

Another, more poised woman might have said, So I've changed my mind. You're not my type. Get lost, soldier. Mary's head ducked farther down and she muttered at her fingers, "I don't want to be one of your conquests!"

AMANDA CARPENTER was raised in South Bend, Indiana, but lived for many years in England. She started writing because she felt a need to communicate with people from other walks of life. She wrote her first romance novel when she was nineteen and has been translated into many languages. Although she has many interests, including music and art, writing is her greatest love.

Books by Amanda Carpenter

HARLEQUIN PRESENTS
1384—PASSAGE OF THE NIGHT
1596—CRY WOLF
1635—A SOLITARY HEART

AMANDA CARPENTER

Perfect Chance

Harlequin Books

TORONTO • NEW YORK • LONDON
AMSTERDAM • PARIS • SYDNEY • HAMBURG
STOCKHOLM • ATHENS • TOKYO • MILAN
MADRID • WARSAW • BUDAPEST • AUCKLAND

ISBN 0-373-11826-0

PERFECT CHANCE

First North American Publication 1996.

This edition published by arrangement with Harlequin Books S.A.

® and TM are trademarks of the publisher. Trademarks indicated with
® are registered in the United States Patent and Trademark Office, the
Canadian Trade Marks Office and in other countries.

Printed in U.S.A.

CHAPTER ONE

MARY paused to lean against the counter of the nurses' station as she surveyed the emergency room in the Newman wing at Memorial Hospital.

It was July 4th, the busiest day of the year.

It was midafternoon and she was already tired, having been on shift since eleven the night before. She rubbed at the back of her neck and thought longingly of the shower she would have when she got home.

Then a fresh influx of people rushed in. Urgent words swirled around and she snatched at a few of them: a boating accident, seven injured, two badly. She darted around a small group of young men who were soaking wet, caught a powerful whiff of beer from them, and rushed toward one of the more serious cases.

A dark-haired girl, maybe six or seven, was being cradled in the arms of an adult. Mary checked her over quickly. The girl had a compound fracture, there was an expertly applied tourniquet above the knee, and she was unconscious. The poor little thing. Her pulse was fluttering and too rapid, her skin ashen under her tan, and she was covered in a cold sweat.

"She's in shock." The deep, gravelly voice sounded overhead.

"I see that. Bring her this way." Mary ran with him over to a cubicle. A sobbing woman tried to follow but was diverted from the front desk by Sandy, who needed her to fill out forms. With relief, Mary heard

Sandy's soothing voice assuring the woman that her daughter was going to be fine.

The man laid the little girl carefully on the gurney, and whipped around to the nearby cabinet. He and Mary collided as they both reached for a blanket at the same time. She whoofed at the impact; it was like running into a brick wall. He snapped, "Why don't you go find a doctor?"

Oh, not again! The top of her head seemed to ignite like a torch. "I am a doctor!"

Some people laughed; some people apologized. This one gave her a hard, narrow-eyed stare and muttered grimly, "You'd better be."

She yanked the blanket out of his hands and shook it over the child. "Get out of my way."

He backed up rapidly. As she prepared an IV, Mary called out sharply, "Julie, I need you."

The nurse came at a run, and together they got the girl stabilized, bandaged and ready for X rays. Mary glanced around for the father. There he was, leaning against the wall, watching everything with hawklike intensity. Overlong blond hair fell into sharp hazel eyes, and his tanned, chiseled face was thoughtful. He's awfully calm, she thought, and she glared at him. No parent should be that calm when his daughter's facing surgery. I'm a doctor and I'm not that calm. What's the matter with him?

She tried to gentle her voice. "What's your daughter's name?"

His attention shifted to her and his eyebrows rose slowly. "Erin Morley. But she's not my daughter. Her mother's out in the lobby."

"Oh." Mary paused. Well, he's still to calm. She asked, "Would you go get her mother? I need to know if Erin is allergic to anything."

"I asked on the way to the hospital. She's not allergic to any medications."

At that moment the mother walked into the cubicle and went to lean against the man, her face streaked and traumatized. The man patted her back soothingly as she confirmed what he'd told Mary, and with the little girl admitted to the hospital, Julie wheeled her gurney to X ray while Mary moved to another patient.

Victor, the other doctor on duty, was still with the other seriously injured patient, a man with a head wound. She passed the cubicle where he was working, sleek dark head bent and handsome features absorbed in his task. He glanced up and nodded to her. She waved back and attended to others from the boating accident, all minor injuries now, listening sympathetically to compulsive telling and retelling of the story.

Mary was a small woman, with a slight, coltish build and delicate, irregular features that made her look far younger than her twenty-six years, but she was capable of a mighty big fury when she was roused to it. Her large blue eyes flashed as she heard of the crash. Four young students had been drinking and driving a speedboat that had collided with a large yacht filled with passengers. She recognized a few faces from the faculty of the local university. They were all very lucky; apparently, due to the quick action of someone on the yacht, there had been no drownings.

Drinking and driving was hardly regulated enough on land to suit Mary. People could have died, and did die in such accidents, and there wasn't even any law to prohibit drunken speedboating. She had been born and raised in Cherry Bay, and had heard many stories similar to the one she heard now. It never failed to outrage her.

The last patient needing attention was one of the drunken young men, waiting sullenly in one of the cubicles. He needed stitches in his arm, and she attended to him in thin-lipped silence.

One of his friends was standing beside him, glowering. Except for their size, they looked like petulant, unrepentant boys.

They were arguing in a heated undertone about the accident. "Didn't I tell you? You should have let me drive," said the one Mary was stitching.

The other one sneered, "Let you drive? For God's sake, Peter, you can't even sit up straight."

"God, my dad is gonna kill me. And you, Trevor—he's gonna kill you, too. Do you know how much that boat cost him? Thirty thousand dollars! How'm I gonna tell him his precious boat is sitting at the bottom of the lake right now?"

The image of the ashen-faced child with the broken leg flashed through Mary's mind, and she controlled the urge to bash both of them over the head with an instrument tray. She finished the job and reached for bandages.

Trevor ran his hands through his damp hair, jerked up his chin and said belligerently, "It wasn't my fault, I tell you. Hell, they swerved in front of me—and anyway, his insurance'll cover it. No problem."

That did it. She slapped down her handful of bandages, rounded on him and said tightly, "Get out."

He ogled her, mouth slack. Then his face flushed, and he said insolently, "Sure thing, sweetie. Soon's you're done patching up my friend here."

She said icily, "My name is not 'sweetie'. My name is Dr. Newman, and I have a job to finish here. The police must be here by now, so why don't you go tell your story to them—or haven't you got it straight yet?"

Alarm registered in Trevor's face and he started to back away. "Maybe I better take off, Pete—"

Fury darkened the other man's cheeks. "And leave me to clean up your mess? No way, dammit—"

He lunged off the gurney toward Trevor, knocking against Mary, who stumbled back, lost her footing, and sat down on the floor so hard her teeth jarred together. Shock held her frozen for a moment, then with a thrill of fear she scrambled to her feet and opened her mouth to shout for help as the two men surged back and forth like prizefighters.

What came next happened so fast all Mary saw was a blur of movement. One moment the two men were grappling each other and cursing, then the next moment Trevor was subdued on the floor, and Peter was back on the gurney where he belonged, with a large, powerful hand locked around his throat. Mary's huge gaze followed the hand back to its owner.

It belonged to a long, lean, hard-muscled body dressed in faded cutoff jeans and a skintight black sleeveless shirt. He stood casually, weight on one slim hip, blond hair in his eyes. He was even smiling a little. She recognized the man who had carried in Erin. Big, he's very big, she thought numbly. I didn't notice that before. And he's *still* calm, but—oh, I don't like the looks of that smile.

"I'm getting a little tired of you two," he remarked
quietly. His sparkling hazel eyes sliced to her, sharp
as a blade. "Are you through with this one, Doctor?"

"I..." She twisted and untwisted her hands, staring.
Somehow the man's presence had such an aura of
settled maturity that he relegated the other two back
to the status of spoiled boys. She worked her aching
jaw, then tried a nervous smile. "Yes. No. I
mean—" Darn it! "He needs a bandage and a prescription for antibiotics."

He looked down at the one on the floor, eyes hard
and deadly. "You're the driver of the boat, aren't you?
I've already given my statement to the police. They're
waiting out front to hear from you. Get." After a
resentful pause, Trevor stood and scurried away. Then
the blond man turned to her. "Why don't you go write
the prescription? I'll stay with this one while a nurse
finishes his bandage."

Mary sucked in a breath and bristled. Don't tell me
what to do! The man cocked his head at her, waiting.
His hand was still locked around Peter's throat. Her
courage wavered when she looked at the drunken
young man, and suddenly she deflated and mumbled,
"Be right back."

Safely back at the nurses' desk, Mary scribbled out
a prescription, pressing down hard with the pen and
slapping it down afterward. Who did that man think
he was? Ordering her about! And those other two—
what criminal stupidity! Worried about a thirty-
thousand-dollar boat, when people could have died!
She wanted to find out how Erin was, she wanted to
sit down and have a cup of coffee and eat that lunch
she hadn't managed to get to, and she wanted a nap.
She looked around. Everything had gone quiet for

now. She took a deep breath, rubbed her face hard with both hands and shuddered.

A hand descended onto her slight shoulder, and she jumped. ''What? Oh—hi, it's you.''

Dr. Victor Prentiss stood looking quizzically down at her. Just under six feet tall, he was a slender, elegant man in his early thirties. Mary had started dating him a few years ago when she was still an intern. A quiet, rather shy, bookish individual, she had been thrilled when Victor had shown an interest in her. Between the pressures of her internship and Victor's career demands, their courtship to date had been sporadic. Now that Mary had started her residency and was working closely with him, she felt it was even uncomfortable at times—she was inexperienced and didn't know how to date a man and also keep a professional distance at work—but she greeted him right now with relief.

''Are you all right?'' Victor asked her gently. ''I heard some of the ruckus.''

''Yes, I'm fine. Just tired. I missed lunch,'' she said miserably. On top of a double shift. Were those black spots in front of her eyes? Squinting, she tried to chase them down.

''The Fourth of July is always like this. Look, darling—it's almost six. Why don't you get some dinner and go home?'' He rubbed her back softly.

''Almost six?'' She looked around in surprise. Where did the time go? Working in the E.R. was always like that. Whenever she came in, it felt like she was entering a twilight zone of crisis after crisis. This was a small community normally, but as a celebrated resort area, the population more than quadrupled in the summer. She had just started working at the E.R. in May but it felt like she had been working there forever, and she could never shake the sneaking suspicion that she was inadequate for the job. Now guilt and gratitude warred for supremacy. "Are you sure?"

"It's quiet now," Victor assured her. "And Kelly is due any minute. Don't drive hungry and tired, though. Go on, get something to eat before you go home. And if you want to call tonight off, I'll understand."

Victor was supposed to be taking her and her younger brother, Tim, to see the fireworks over Lake Michigan that evening. She had been looking forward to it once, but now, with every bone in her feet and legs aching, it didn't sound nearly as fun as it had. "I'll think about it. I did promise Tim, though...." Her voice trailed off as she caught sight of Peter being marched toward the nurses' station by the bossy blond man, who still wore an unpleasant smile as he kept a firm grip on Peter's newly bandaged arm.

Mary felt herself compact into the smallest possible package. It didn't make her invisible, however. The two men stopped in front of her, and there was an uncomfortable pause. Then the blond man said lazily, "You got something to say, Pete?"

The younger fellow studied his shoes and muttered, "I'm sorry."

Mary glanced around. Victor watched the tableau with detached interest. In contrast, the blond man's hard features were distinctly wicked. One of the nurses audibly suppressed a chuckle. Hazel eyes flickered in that direction, a thoroughly male glance, and grew very bright. He said, "You're sorry, what?"

"I'm sorry, Doctor," Peter amended quickly.

Why is my face hot? she wondered. She scrambled for something intelligent and dignified to say, snatched up the prescription and thrust it at him. "Go away."

Victor took up the slack smoothly, moving around the nurses' desk and taking Peter's other arm with a smile. "Dr. Newman has been under a lot of stress." He led the young man away, talking quietly, his tone commiserating.

Mary blinked down at her hands, face growing even warmer. Ah. She shouldn't be rude to the patients, no matter how she felt about them. No matter what they'd done. Maybe the ground would open up right then and there, swallow her up, and she could have a nap in the hole.

That man was still standing there.

Don't look up, she told herself.

Maybe he'll go away, too.

Maybe I can pretend I dropped something here, behind the nurses' desk. She frowned professionally at the floor and bent down suddenly. There was a long silence. No footsteps sounded, leading away. He's still up there and now I'm down here. What next? She opened a cabinet and started rummaging through it. Inventory, maybe. Residents always do inventory after their shifts. Sure they do.

Silence. Her white coat was terribly hot and scratchy. She pulled at her collar.

Don't look up.

"Dr. Newman?" That man. He sounded amused.

She felt herself cringe, and her gaze crept up slowly. He leaned against the counter, tanned biceps bulging. Big, he was, and—and so male. Calmly male. That long, sexy mouth held in a crooked smile. Her glance bounced off it, up to his gaze, and skittered away.

"Y-yes?" She straightened reluctantly. "Hi, you're still there."

The skin around his eyes crinkled. He wasn't a terribly young man, maybe in his mid- to late-thirties. That was a knowledgeable, worldly, terrifying face. "And so are you," he observed.

She was hot, sticky, scratchy, her teeth and legs hurt, and her stomach was howling for food. One hand crept up self-consciously to her tangled, waist-length mane of hair that was pulled back in a ponytail. It was crooked. She had absolutely no idea what to say to him. "Er—is there something I can do for you?"

"Yes, I heard you were going to get some dinner. Would you mind showing me where the cafeteria is?"

"Oh! That's easy—you just go down the hall, then take a right to the elevators, and—"

His slow, deep voice, smooth as melted chocolate, cut her off. "I'm terrible with directions."

Her hand, which had been busy gesturing, fluttered back to hide balled in her pocket. "A-are you? I see. Well." She didn't have time for this. If she didn't get something to eat soon, she was going to faint. As if on cue, her stomach rumbled loudly. She gave the man a weak smile and gave in. He knew she was going that way anyway. How churlish could she get? "Of course I'll show you."

His smile deepened subtly at the corners. "Thank you."

He waited while she retrieved her purse from the doctors' lounge, and then fell into step beside her. Mary looked down at the floor and watched their legs, his legs, those long, bare, gold-dusted legs with the smooth, rolling stride. Lord, he had to be well over six feet tall. And she was only five foot two. She took three steps for every one of his, like a chihuahua trotting beside a Great Dane.

She pulled up short, and he stopped, too. "I—are you sure you wouldn't like to go on ahead? I'd like to find out how the little girl you brought in is doing."

"Erin's doing fine," he said. "She's out of surgery, and the surgeon that worked on her says she'll be good as new in a couple of months."

"Oh," she said, and her tired face broke into a smile. "That's good news."

"Yes, she was lucky." He hesitated, looking down at her, something odd in his expression. Then he said, "I stayed with her mother until Erin's father could get here."

Mary had turned to start walking again. It was a few moments before what he said sank in, then her head swiveled toward him suspiciously. Is he doing what I think he's doing? "I see?" No! That wasn't supposed to be a question.

"They're married, you know," he said. "Erin's parents, I mean."

Her eyes grew round. Yes, she thought, I think he is. "Ah?"

He twinkled. "Happily."

He's flirting! Or—maybe teasing. She scrabbled madly for a change of subject. "By the way, did you tell me your name?"

He chuckled outright and ran a long-fingered hand through his hair. "Nope. It's Chance. What's yours?"

"Mary," she replied automatically.

There's something wrong with this scene, she thought distractedly. Chance. What a name. He should have a leather jacket and a motorcycle, maybe a tattoo or two, and I—well, I don't fit at all. A vision occurred to her, one of a big, busty blonde in a skin-tight minidress cooing on his arm. Yes, that would be more like it. She scowled with relief as they reached the large, well-appointed cafeteria. There now, we can each buy our food and go our separate ways.

"Well, here we are!" she said cheerfully, and she mentally dismissed him as they got into line. The smell of hot food hit her hard, and she piled things greedily onto her tray. Breakfast had been a year ago. She took lasagna, salad, a banana, chocolate cake, milk and coffee, paid for her meal and wandered away to find a place to sit.

As she settled in her seat, a shadow fell across her plates and she looked up. Chance stood there, laden tray in one hand, the other resting on the chair beside her. He said brightly, "Mind if I join you?"

Well, what could she say? "No, of course not," she mumbled, and she watched him put his dishes on the table beside her. Lasagna, salad, a banana, chocolate cake, milk and coffee. Oh . . . She sucked in a breath. Was that weird? That looked a little weird to her. She wondered if she knew anybody here that was bigger than he was.

She looked around, pale under her warm summer tan, dark shadows smudged under her eyes, seeming so wan and forlorn that the man who sat beside her took pity on her and said gently, "I thought, since you worked here, you'd know what was good to eat. Cafeteria food can be—chancy, if you don't mind a bad pun."

That sounded so reasonable, she threw a smile blindly in his general direction, ducked her head and ate. Gradually the world, which had started to spin slowly around on her, stabilized and became real again. Colors, and sounds, and the fake plants in the section dividers came into focus.

Chance had seemed content enough with the companionable silence. When she had sucked down the last of her milk and was cradling her coffee cup in both hands, Mary dared to pick up the conversation again. "So," she said, "how did you get involved with the boating accident?"

"I was on the yacht, the *Gypsy Dancer*." With neat, economical movements, he polished off the last of his cake.

"I know that boat. The dean owns it." She'd been on the yacht once, at a graduation party. Harold Schubert, dean of the university, was known among certain circles for his annual Fourth of July yacht party. She felt a twinge of regret for the boat's smooth, clean lines. "Was it badly damaged?"

Chance shrugged and grimaced. "Well, we got to shore, but she was taking on water. She's in better shape than that speedboat, though."

"I heard that went under."

"Yeah, what was left of it." Remnants of anger smoldered briefly in his eyes.

Mary shuddered. "Erin wasn't the only one who was lucky. All of you were."

He glanced at her. "I know it. Those idiots. We couldn't have gotten out of their way. The *Dancer* had some real pretty moves on the water, but no thirty-foot yacht can turn that fast."

Mary settled back in her chair, eyelids drooping as she considered him. Her stomach felt stretched too full and she was getting sleepy. She'd heard something else about the crash. What was it? Thanks to someone's quick thinking, no one had drowned. Well, this man was quick. She could certainly attest to that after witnessing him defuse the situation back in the E.R. She wondered if he had been the one people had talked about. "Oh, I meant to thank you for stopping that fight."

He angled his head toward her, elbows on the table. "I figured you were busy enough without having to sew those two back together. Otherwise, I might have just let them kill each other. Damned selfish fools."

However she might agree with that sentiment, she felt uncomfortable about voicing it, especially after Victor had interceded for her when she lost control earlier. She shifted in her seat. She asked with diffident curiosity, "So are you friends with Harold?" She tried to imagine it, but couldn't quite. Harold was so urbane, a natural politician who dealt dexterously with not only the university set of Cherry Bay, but the native population, both the country-club set and the working class, and the summer tourists, as well. On the other hand, Chance apparently wasn't a man to mince words.

His eyebrows rose. "Harold? You're on a first-name basis with old Shoe-Licking Schubert?"

Mary tried hard not to spit coffee. Grabbing quickly for her napkin, she covered her mouth and coughed, eyes watering. Chance pounded her on the back, until she waved her hands at him to stop. "Well," she wheezed emphatically, "that's a—refreshing point of view."

"It's the truth."

He was still eyeing her inquiringly, so she cleared her throat and told him, "Harold—" Licks my grandfather's shoes, she nearly said, but caught herself quickly and changed a chortle into another cough.

"Ahem! Harold and my grandfather are acquaintances. He and his wife have been for dinner."

The realization registered very quickly with him. His gaze flickered and then went opaque. Did the bit of news pique his interest, or kill it? It was hard to tell. Neither option was good. And was she disappointed? Though she worked hard, she couldn't come up with an answer to that, and her transparent face, as always, registered everything that went on inside her. His eyes narrowed. "Ah, so you're one of those Newmans, are you?"

One shoulder lifted and rotated in a fine show of indifference. "So what if I am?" Of course I don't care. Why would I care, for heaven's sake? And besides, Victor's going to find out I ate dinner with this man and be—be what, jealous? She tried hard to get there, to picture Victor jealous, then just sagged in her seat. No, he'd be surprised.

Her fork was out of line with her knife. She straightened it carefully. Out of her vision, Chance's face broke into a predatory grin. He forced it away and said evenly, "I don't know that Schubert and I are friends, but as a member of the faculty, I get invited to his parties now and then."

Her little face tilted up and brightened as she snatched at that conversational tidbit. "You're a member of the faculty? What do you teach?" It couldn't be anything to do with medicine, or Mary would have heard of him or seen him by now.

"Journalism."

"Oh." That was clever repartee, Mary. She shut her mouth firmly and stole sideways glances at him. She felt as if she was looking at a different, rather dangerous, species in fascination. He didn't strike her as the academic type. She couldn't see him as a career professor and wondered what kind of journalist he would make. No doubt a very good one; she had firsthand experience of his tenacity.

Something danced in his eyes. "You don't have to be worried. I won't bite." His voice dropped to a seductive purr. "At least, not without permission."

This time she felt not only her eyes round, but her mouth, too. He was back to flirting, or teasing, and either one was frightening. He was a creature so very far out of her sphere of existence, she felt instinctively that the wisest course of action would be to throw her coat over her head and run for cover. He lounged back in his chair, a sleek, honed machine, and his heavy-lidded gaze traveled slumberously over her. She felt as if she had been physically touched by psychic tendrils that curled around her body and crooned of male intent.

Like a spider wrapping up its dinner in a cocoon.

She gulped. Now was the time to say something witty. "I have to go home," she whispered. "It was nice visiting with you."

Nice?

He unfolded from the chair and stood. She watched him go up—and up—and found her gaze at a level with the skintight shirt that rippled over an accordion stomach. She lunged to her feet and grabbed her purse.

"Do you have a ride home?" Chance asked her. "Because if you'll pardon me for saying so, Dr. Mary, you don't seem to be in any condition to drive."

"I'm all right."

"But it's been a long shift for you, hasn't it?" he asked shrewdly. "And the traffic is worse on land than it is on the lake."

"Well . . ." she said reluctantly, fiddling with the strap of her purse. He did have a point. Even standing made her body groan, and the floor didn't seem any too certain underneath her feet. "Maybe I can get a ride from someone else going off duty."

"I'd be happy to drive you."

I don't know you, she almost said, but she bit it back. No doubt he was just making a generous offer, but every sultry movement and suggestive smile screamed danger. "Thanks, but I'm sure I'll manage."

"Let me make sure you've got a ride at least."

"If there isn't anyone who can take me, I can always get a cab."

He smiled. "On the Fourth of July? You might as well hope for a ride on the space shuttle. Come on, Dr. Mary, your caution is praiseworthy, but I really am just a pussycat. Look—there's old Shoe-Licking Schubert right now. He'll tell you I'm okay."

A pussycat, my belly button, she thought. More like a great prowling hunting cat, preening its whiskers with a Cheshire grin. But she followed his gesture toward the dinner line anyway.

The dean of the university, a slim, balding man in his late fifties, dressed smartly in deck shorts and a blue shirt, stood in line with a few other members of the faculty. They all looked sunburned, tired, and one of them had a bandaged wrist. Mary shifted from foot to foot. "I should go to say hello anyway," she decided out loud.

Chance promptly took her hand, tucked it into the crook of his arm, and led her over to the dean and the others. Mary felt the heat from his bare skin burn into her fingers the entire way.

Harold looked up as they neared and immediately smiled. "Armstrong, good to see you. Why, hello, Mary."

As she returned his greeting, Mary felt more than relief at finding out that Chance was as legitimate as he had promised—was there perhaps some excitement? She scowled. No! He'd just offered her a ride home, for heaven's sake!

Pleasantries were exchanged, but when Harold and the others thanked Chance, apparently again, for all that he'd done after the accident, he suddenly developed an urgent need to leave the scene. Before Mary knew it, they had said their goodbyes and she was being hustled down the corridor away from the cafeteria.

I knew it, she thought, looking up at his face as she trotted to keep up with him. I knew it would take a lot to knock you off your feet. And you don't feel comfortable with the praise, do you? She said in all sincerity, "You're quite the hero today, aren't you?"

He threw her a frowning glance. "I'm no hero. Just some things needed to be done, that's all." Then, before she had time to even consider that as a rebuff, his mood changed entirely. "And I can drive and everything," he added with a wink. "See what a nice pussycat I am? Let me take you home, Doc. That'll be my last good deed for the day, I promise."

Her soft laugh bubbled out. "All right," she said, feeling mighty reckless. Bad though he might be, he was good medicine for her weary psyche. "Thank you."

He had left his car in the parking lot just outside the E.R. entrance, so they walked back the way they had come. Kelly, Mary's replacement, had indeed arrived and things still didn't look too busy. Maybe the worst of it was over. There would be another rush tonight after the bars closed, but thankfully, several other doctors had volunteered their time for that shift.

She was going home on the arm of a rakish, unpredictable stranger. While it probably shouldn't be giving her the thrill that it was and afterward her life would return to its normal placidity, she was still just happy to be going home.

As they passed the doctors' lounge, Victor, who was relaxing on a couch with a cup of coffee, looked up. He caught sight of Mary, still arm in arm with Chance, and his eyebrows shot up before his fine-boned face went carefully blank.

Yes, she thought resignedly, he was surprised.

She suspected she might have some explaining to do.

CHAPTER TWO

MARY stepped outside, and Chance followed her. The early evening was beautiful, the wide sky clear and the distant, rolling trees hazed in sunlight.

Going from the hospital's air-conditioned coolness into eighty-degree weather was an abrupt shock, though. It was making her heart pound, she decided, pausing to swipe tawny bangs off her forehead. The ponytail had slipped farther, and she dragged out the rubber band, shook out her thick, wavy mane of hair and swiftly put it up again. It wasn't so much blond as tricolored, darker underneath but streaked so light by the sun it was almost platinum in places.

Chance watched, eyes gleaming, the fine lines at his eyes deepening as he squinted in the sun.

She frowned, trying to ignore her self-consciousness from being so closely observed, and asked, "So—how long have you been teaching?"

He indicated which way they were to walk, and they started across the parking lot. Foraging gulls scattered. Even though it was miles from the lake, the hospital nearly always had gulls around. "Ever since I came back to the States and decided to stay in one place for a while."

"How long have you been back in the States?" she asked curiously.

"Just under a year." He smiled at her crookedly, eyes twinkling. "And I've been meeting the most intriguing people."

They reached a black Jeep Cherokee and Chance moved to the passenger door to unlock it. Mary watched the way his hair curled under at the nape of his neck, the balletic fluidity of the muscles in his wide, strong back and shoulders. His legs went on forever. Next to him, she felt very small and inexperienced. Maybe he wasn't so much flirting, but teasing her, as she thought he might be. It was a horrible supposition.

She had no illusions about what she was. Bookish, gawky, she always felt like a duck out of water at any of the social gatherings her family was invited to because of their standing in the local community and their money. Maybe Chance's offer to take her home was how he would treat a baby sister.

By the time Chance had swung around to face her again, she was frowning up at the sky, apparently watching a gull with fierce intensity.

He peered up at the sky, as well, then back down at her. Something curious was going on inside her; it showed in her transparent features. "Hey," he said. "What's up, Doc?"

Her attention came back to him, and she blinked. He was watching her with that crooked, sexy smile. She didn't know why the corners of her mouth drooped.

"Are you teasing me, or flirting?" she burst out, and was immediately mortified. Her cheeks flamed, and she glanced down at her hands. She was holding her purse in front of her like a barrier, shoulders hunched.

Chance regarded her for a moment in fascination. Such a defensive, artless little thing she was. This bundle of awkward nerves was a world apart from the self-assured young doctor who earlier had told him so authoritatively to get out of her way. He had an innately cynical way of viewing the world, but she was outside his definitions. He doubted she could lie to save her own life.

She had removed her white coat, and what she wore underneath were simple buttercup yellow dungarees and a white T-shirt with a scooped neckline. The outfit was bright, cheerful and unsophisticated. The scooped neckline showed collarbones as fragile and as gracefully formed as butterfly wings.

He took a step forward and slid long, hard fingers lightly under her chin, tilting up her face. The shock of the touch was unmistakably intimate. "Oh, I'm definitely flirting," he murmured, unable to resist rubbing the ball of his callused thumb across those velvet-soft, astonished lips.

She gaped at him, sensual alarm bells in her body clanging wildly. His thumb stroked her mouth unhurriedly, hazel eyes gleaming with pleasure. Every sensible notion inside her flapped away on the breeze, and she stood shivering, open to any possibility.

He was going to kiss her. He was going to devour her. How incredibly, frightfully delicious.... He dropped his hand and stepped back, opening the car door for her. She blinked, breathing hard and still trembling. It was time to get in the car. The car, Mary. Going home, Mary. Remember? With a crash of air castles and expectations, she got into the seat. The Jeep sat high off the ground, and it was an unexpected stretch up. She practically had to climb to get in.

As Chance prowled around the back of the Jeep to the driver's side, she numbly fumbled for her seat belt.

Her fingers seemed made of putty, while a sense of anticlimax leadened her mind.

She didn't know the rules of this game. She'd never played it before. Why hadn't he kissed her? Because he was just flirting? But she had wanted him to flirt earlier, flirting being far better than teasing. What the hell was the matter with her?

Chance slid smoothly into the driver's seat, and started the engine. Mary watched him and wondered what it would feel like, to have his mouth on hers.

His head angled toward her, eyes gone dark. All hint of amused lightness was gone, and he was shuttered, withdrawn. He took a pair of sunglasses from the visor and slipped them on. "Where do you live?"

Her brows twitched together. What was this? Absently, she gave him directions, and he backed the Jeep out of the parking space.

The Newman estate was located about twelve miles out of town, in a quiet, wooded stretch of land that Mary's great-grandfather had bought at the turn of the century. Hugh Newman had determined early in his life to establish a dynasty and had made his fortune in the shipping business. He had passed the business on to his son, Wallis, and had died a contented man, secure in the knowledge that he had fulfilled his dream and that his descendants were going to continue being a major power in the country indefinitely.

Four generations later, it was an entirely different story. Mary's entire family consisted of her fourteen-year-old brother, Tim, and her grandfather, Wallis, who was in his mid-eighties and in delicate health. Wallis sold the shipping business when his son and daughter-in-law died, and has spent the latter years of his life devoted to his two grandchildren.

Chance navigated smoothly through the crowded downtown streets, swung past the university complex, and they quickly reached the highway that skirted the bay. Half of the trip home was conducted in silence. Mary stared out the window at the familiar scenery, the sparkling blue water to her right and the rolling hills on the left, unable to shake a sense of letdown.

I'm tired, she thought. That's all it is. No sleep the night before, and now I have to decide if I have the energy to go to the fireworks like I promised Tim. The thought of spending several hours in the company of Victor and her younger brother was vaguely depressing.

Chance glanced at her broodingly. The sound of his low voice in the confines of the Jeep was startling. "You awake?"

"Hunh?" She shook herself out of her reverie. "Oh, yes. Sorry—I was drifting."

"That's all right. You had a long day."

"I went on shift last night at eleven." She knuckled dry, scratchy eyes. "It's hard to believe sometimes that I've only been a resident for a couple of months. That on top of my internship makes it seem like I've been doing double shifts my whole life, and I still have so far to go."

"Well, I've heard residency's pretty tough. Kind of like boot camp for doctors. You like it?"

She smiled but it was fleeting. Did she like it? "Does anybody like boot camp?"

He chuckled. "Good point. There must be a sense of satisfaction when you're doing your best, but it's not the same as liking it, is it?"

She sighed, and was rather disturbed at how heavy and dispirited it sounded. "No, it isn't."

He reached out and covered her hands briefly, and she stared down at the large, square back of his hand, the tanned skin sprinkled with golden hairs and webbed gracefully with veins. Sinewed, strong, the tapered fingers sensitive; she liked his hands. "You sound awfully unhappy, Dr. Mary. Why are you doing it?"

From nowhere a pressure welled up inside her, and suddenly the urge to confide in someone, a stranger who had no expectations of her and no demands, became irresistible. She sighed again. "I had good reasons once. I think I still do. I love taking care of people, especially children. I love seeing them get better and knowing I'm one of the reasons why. It's just that sometimes I wonder if I've gone about doing it the right way."

Everybody was so supportive of her. Her grandfather had encouraged her every step of the way. Victor had offered her lots of guidance in her career choices. Even Tim had brought her coffee and rubbed her shoulders during late-night study sessions when she had been in medical school. She couldn't let them down, not after all that they'd done for her.

It's just that she wondered sometimes when she was going to find time for her own life. Sure, she wanted to take care of people, but when was she going to get the chance to take care of her own children? After two frenetic years of residency would come a busy career.

The times when she and Victor had talked cautiously about a possible future together, he had always evinced satisfaction with how things were going. He liked the idea of having a wife who was as career oriented as he was. He liked the respect and prestige, and the life-style. Lots of people managed two demanding professions in their relationships. Was that too much to ask?

Chance said quietly, "It's easy to get bogged down in a career and forget you're a human being."

Mary turned to look at him. He looked so remote, attention trained on the road, half of his expression covered by the dark glasses. Was he talking about her, or himself? A career in journalism, traveling all over the world—how many opportunities could he have had for a normal life, wife, kids.

Good Lord—could he be married? With an awful feeling in the pit of her stomach, she sneaked a look at his left hand. No ring, and no tan line, either. But some men didn't wear rings.

If he was in his late thirties, he could have three or four marriages by now, and any number of kids. Mary could just picture them, blond hair dripping into their sad eyes, wanting their daddy to stop flirting with her and come home to them. She gritted her teeth, revolted by the image.

Now, wait a minute. Find a nice roundabout way to ask him. "Have you—found time for a career and maybe marriage, too?"

His lips twitched. "Plenty of career, but no marriage. Not yet. I'm one of those men that got bogged down. One day I got home, walked into my apartment in New York, and everything was covered in dust. No food in the fridge. Hell, I couldn't even keep a cat. Everybody I knew was a work contact. I'd lost touch with most of my friends years ago. That was when I decided to slow down. Nobody ought to work that hard."

Her depression stopped riding her shoulders and blew out the window, and she gave him a sunny smile. "I thought about becoming a pediatrician, but that would be four more years of training on top of what I'm doing now. And then I'd spend all my time taking care of other people's children."

"And when would you find time to have any fun?" he asked dryly. "Let alone have any children of your own."

"Well," she said self-consciously, "yes." So what. She could admit that she wanted children. That was a perfectly reasonable desire. A lot of people wanted children; it wasn't as if she was hinting at anything.

And fun. What a pretty, simple, three-letter word that was, but what a concept. When was the last time she could say to herself, gee, I had fun?

Then the realization shook through her: she didn't have any idea whether Victor wanted children or not. That was such an elemental knowledge of another person, but in the two years they had gone out together, the subject had never come up. And Mary couldn't even make a good guess based on what she knew of his personality.

Victor and she were practically engaged. He was certainly by far the most serious relationship she'd ever had. In college she'd dated a few times, but she was mostly preoccupied with her schoolwork and her brother, who had needed her to be a surrogate mother. He didn't even remember their parents, who had died in a car crash when she was seventeen and Tim was only five. She hadn't had time for more than casual relationships, but Victor, who was also a doctor, and understood the stresses of her life, had pursued her with patience. She'd not only been flattered by his attention, but comforted by the companionship.

They reached the turnoff and began the long drive through the wooded twenty-acre estate to the large house. The clock on the Jeep's dashboard read almost eight o'clock. The sun had set behind the tree line, and it was growing dark. Chance removed his sunglasses, pulled the Jeep to a stop, and regarded the sprawling manor house with raised eyebrows. Some of the windows were well lit, but the shadows outside were spiky and dark.

"You live in that?"

Mary started to chuckle. "Yes," she said, "I know. It's a monstrosity, isn't it? But my great-grandfather was so proud of it."

"There're about three or four different plans going on. What's it look like from the back?"

"Worse. There're a couple of pavilions, an overgrown topiary garden, an arched bridge that doesn't span anything, an unsuccessful artificial pond that turned to swamp around World War II and a rotting boathouse. It must have been something in the roaring twenties, but now it's a little sad, like an abandoned carnival. Every two years or so, my grandfather swears he's going to tear it down and build something more sensible."

"I saw something like it in a horror movie once. All these college kids were being chased around by a maniac with a meat cleaver." He cocked his head. "I don't think I could sleep in that place."

She covered her mouth and giggled at the image of such a tough, self-reliant man huddled wide awake in bed with the night sweats. "It's not so bad when you've been raised in it. Then you don't know anything different, you see. I always hoped to find a secret passage, but I never did. The attic is a wonderful place to play on a rainy day. It's huge and filled with all kinds of junk.''

He shook his head, smiling, and opened his door. The song of crickets and the fresh smell of the woods filled the night air. Mary opened her door, as well, then realized that he was coming around to her side of the Jeep.

She looked up at him, her heart starting another idiotic tap dance. The creases on either side of his mouth were deepened by his smile, and he reached out for her with both hands. ''Such a fancy manor house,'' he drawled, twin devils laughing in his eyes. ''It must be bringing out the genteel in me.''

Eyes riveted to his reckless face, she held out her hands, but instead of taking hold of them, he took her by the waist and lifted her lightly out of the Jeep. At some point her feet touched the ground. She wasn't sure when; all of her attention had plummeted to the warm, firm grasp of his hands that nearly spanned her middle.

They stood very close together. Somehow her hands had found their way to grip his upper arms. The heat from his lean torso and legs radiated through her light cotton dungarees, and she caught the merest hint of his scent, clean and redolent of fresh air and very male.

Mary was fixated, electrified. At no time during her sheltered life had she experienced anything like the sensations that rioted through her. The shape of his down-bent head against the sky was a hieroglyph with archetypical meaning, and the shadowed, intent expression on his face made her stare in wonder.

Chance murmured, "Walk you to the door, Mary?"

It was so old-fashioned. Genteel. She was enchanted. "Thank you," she breathed. "Oh, and thank you for bringing me home, too."

"My pleasure." After holding her a pulsing moment too long, he turned and slid one hand to the small of her back as they strolled to the porch. "I've enjoyed meeting you."

"Me, too." She stared at the steps hard, willing herself to negotiate them properly and not do something stupid like trip and fall flat on her face. That was hard to do when her knees seemed to have a mind of their own. They paused at the door.

"Are you planning to go watch the fireworks on the beach tonight, or are you calling it a day?"

"I—haven't made up my mind yet." She wasn't that tired after all. The celebration didn't start until ten. She could have some more coffee, a shower, maybe a quick nap, and she got to sleep in as late as she liked tomorrow. Just an hour or two, for Tim's sake. "Are you going?"

"I thought I might." His low voice was somewhere between gravel and velvet, a fascinating combination: dangerous and smooth. "Perhaps I'll see you there, then."

"That'd—that'd be nice."

Nice?

He had never removed the hand from her back. Now he brought up the other one and stroked her cheek lightly with the back of his fingers. The sensation was so liquid, so gentle, she nearly melted into a puddle at his feet. Then, slowly, his head came down and his mouth covered hers.

Her eyelids drifted closed, and the world went somewhere else, as the shape and the pressure of his mouth eclipsed everything. After a long, timeless moment, gripped by some mysterious suspense, she parted her lips and touched her tongue to him, and tasted him. He tasted like fresh air and something else, something that was entirely, uniquely himself.

Then his hand shifted to cradle the back of her head, and he kissed her deeply. His tongue thrust into her mouth and stroked at hers, delving in hard, and she moaned in surprise, in delight.

This is what it all means, this explosion of flavor and intensity of feeling; she kissed him back, eagerly, shakily, falling into this new eroticism and drowning in it.

Chance sucked in a hissing breath, pulling back just long enough to stare at her with eyes that glittered hot like a raptor's, and then he plunged down again and ravished her mouth.

She clung to his shoulders mindlessly. He had turned her inside out, and all her nerve endings were raw, exposed to the warm summer breeze. When he ran his hand up her back to press her closer against his body, it was like being jolted with a strong electric current.

"...why haven't you come in yet—hey! Mary? Who the hell are you kissing?"

The young, imperious voice penetrated her heated mind slowly. It apparently did the same for Chance, who lifted his head. She made the oddest, most shocking sound when his mouth left hers. It sounded so needy, so like a whimper. Through blurred eyes, she saw his nostrils flare, and his hand, at the nape of her neck, spasmed tight in an instinctively possessive grip.

Two observations, then: Tim was at the front door, now sounding offended. And she was clinging to Chance like a limpet. She dropped hold of him fast, they fell away from each other, and she turned to Tim defensively.

"Why—why—are you spying on me, Tim?" She was having trouble getting her breath back. God, she was having trouble getting any kind of presence of mind back.

She turned to look at Chance, who had whipped away, putting his back to the two of them. As she watched, he ran both hands through his hair, pivoted back toward the scene again, and regarded Tim's lanky frame with narrowed eyes. "Who the hell are you?" he demanded.

She watched shock go over Tim's bony face. Then the boy drew himself up very tall—and he was, too, much taller than she was—and he shot back snottily, "I'm her brother, you moron."

"Tim!" Mary exclaimed in a shocked voice. He stalked over to wrap a skinny, protective arm around her, glaring at the intruder.

"And Victor's on the phone for you," Tim added pointedly to her.

Chance put his hands on his hips. He looked composed again, almost remote, except that his eyes were dilated black as sin, and his expression was tight. "Who the hell is Victor?"

"Her fiancé," snapped Tim defiantly.

Mary sputtered as she ogled her brother. "What has gotten into you?" she demanded. Then she said emphatically to Chance, "He's just a friend!"

Chance frowned sharply. "I thought you said you were her brother."

"I am!"

"No, I mean Victor!" she exclaimed.

His eyebrows shot up. Was that an evil gleam in his eye? "Victor is your brother?"

"No, he's her fiancé!"

"He is not!" She punched Tim in the side. "Timothy, stop it! Victor is just a friend. This little demon is my brother."

"Your very protective brother, I see." Chance stepped forward and held out his hand. "I'm Chance Armstrong. I gave your sister a ride home from the hospital."

"Chance?" muttered Tim, his leery gaze sliding sideways to hers. Something undefinable seemed to pass between the man and the boy. Mary couldn't decipher it. Whatever it was, it was decidedly a male thing, something in Chance's unwavering, cool gaze that made Tim's bristling slowly die down. He reached out uncertainly and received a firm, no-nonsense handshake from the older man. "I, er, how d'you do?"

Oh, now he remembers his manners, she thought distractedly. But she noticed Tim still hadn't let go of her.

Chance looked at Mary and gave her a nod. "I'd better be going," he said quietly. "See you later?"

"I—yes, see you later." She held out her hand. He gave her fingers a brief, hard squeeze, and then he strolled down the steps and to his Jeep.

Tim led Mary inside. She watched over her shoulder as the Jeep's headlights came on and Chance drove away.

"Mary? What are you looking at? You were really kissing that guy. I've never seen you do that. Did you forget what I said? Victor's on the phone—unless he's hung up by now."

"Hunh?" Mary murmured dreamily. "Oh, of course."

Tim was right. She'd never been kissed like that before. What kind of a kiss was that anyway? It was the kind that sucked your soul out of your body.

Hey, she wanted to call out to the man who'd just left. You forgot to give my soul back.

Instead she went in to answer the phone.

Some time later...

"Mary?" Tim's voice. "I brought you coffee like you asked. Mary, are you awake?"

She fought her way out of a black hole, toward wakefulness and the sound of her brother's voice. "Mmm, 's the coffee. Oh, thank you, baby." She lifted her head off the pillow, eyes still glued shut, and he kissed her face several times.

One thing she cherished about Tim was that they had always shared an uncommonly close bond, and he was unusual for a prickly fourteen-year-old boy, because he'd never become self-conscious about physical displays of affection. If anything, Tim hovered too much.

Look at how he'd barged out onto the porch earlier that evening, for example. The memory boiled out of the mud in her head, and she groaned.

She tried her mouth again, and this time it worked a little better. "I've got to shower. I'll never wake up, Timmy, if I don't get a shower."

"I'll get the shower going, so the water's nice and hot for you," he crooned, and her bed bounced as he leaped up to lope away.

He was so excited. Mary sat up, stretched, and yawned so hard it felt like her jaw cracked. Last year Tim had gone to the fireworks celebration with his best friend's family, but this year the Thompsons were on vacation in Florida, and he had nobody else to go with but her. And he was too young to go by himself.

Tim bounced back into her bedroom. "It's ready! And Victor's going to be here in half an hour."

She winced at his too-loud voice. "Okay, Tim. Thank you. Go on now, let me get ready—and remember, we're only going to stay until midnight. Victor's only had a nap, and mine wasn't long enough—"

"I know, I know," he interrupted. "A couple of hours'll be great. Just get moving, or we'll miss the beginning."

He left, and Mary shuffled around her large, comfortable bedroom, feeling like an old woman. Rescue workers could go weeks on five-minute naps every three or four hours—she could surely make it through the evening after her hour nap. After several minutes in a refreshing cool shower, she was feeling more like herself again. It wouldn't be for long, and it was going to be—*fun*.

As a graduation present from her grandfather, Mary'd had her bathroom and bedroom redecorated. She stepped out of the shower into a pretty collection of greens and peaches. She quickly made up her face, applying blusher, eye shadow and mascara lightly, and then she dithered over which perfume she wanted to use.

Why are you going to so much trouble? she asked herself suddenly. She stared hard at her bright-eyed reflection. Victor's seen you at your worst many times.

You know why, Mary, and it's not for Victor.

It was because of that kiss, because of a "maybe see you later" kind of arrangement with a man you hardly know, a man who's way out of your league, you've admitted that much. A man probably just playing around—what if he kisses everybody like that? A man who is just—flirting.

And what's more, if you'd had your wits about you earlier when you had Victor on the phone, you would have called off the evening with him and gone ahead to the fireworks with Tim. Alone.

Have you gone insane?

The lecture wasn't working. No matter how sternly she talked to herself, the excited young woman in the mirror didn't calm down. She selected at random a perfume bottle from her collection on a nearby shelf, and sprayed some on her neck and wrists. Then she waltzed into her bedroom, humming—what to wear? Oh, a soft, flowered linen skirt with a matching rose sleeveless top, delicate sandals and a plain gold necklace. And the hair, oh, leave it loose and fluff it out, all nice and pretty, there.

You should be wearing shorts, fool.

I don't care, I don't care.

What if he's not there? She stopped in midwaltz and her shoulders drooped. Two long hours, and Victor's going to think you dressed up for him. Oh my. Both hands crept up to her face. And what if he wants to kiss you?

Tim. Tim will be there. Victor wouldn't want to embarrass him. That'll be all right.

What if he does show up? She started to dance again, then stopped dead in her tracks.

How are you going to explain Chance to Victor, Mary? How are you going to explain Victor to Chance?

She caught sight of another reflection from the full-length closet mirror, and she scowled. How, in God's name, did a shy, gawky thing like you find herself in the middle of such a soap opera?

Off in the distance, she heard the front doorbell ring. Victor had arrived.

What are you going to do now, Mary?

CHAPTER THREE

CHERRY Bay's annual Fourth of July celebration was held at the old lighthouse, which was on a promontory of land that had been established as a local park some years ago. Volunteer firemen were in charge of the fireworks display that was set off from the point. The nearby beach was crowded with both natives and tourists alike, and food and drink vendors dotted the area with striped canvas canopies. Music from a local band blared from the loudspeakers near the whitewashed stone lighthouse, and the smell of hot dogs and the pastry called fried elephant ears filled the air.

Tim appeared not to notice the taut atmosphere that filled the interior of Victor's Volvo on the trip to the lighthouse, but Mary did. Back at the house, she had met Victor at the door; he was dressed in crisp linen slacks and a white shirt. She'd looked up into his cold eyes and tight features and felt her stomach sink to her shoes.

When Tim had come to the porch to interrupt Chance and Mary, he had left the phone off the hook in the front hall. How much of what had gone on outside had Victor overheard? Could he have heard anything at all? Could his tight expression just possibly be related to seeing her walk out of the hospital earlier that day with a strange man? What did she dare hope for?

With the strong instinct that she was making a mistake, Mary had gone to say goodbye to her grandfather Wallis, who was comfortably ensconced in the library with an old friend of his, drinking brandy and playing a game of chess.

"Good night, Grampa," she whispered as she kissed him.

A tall, thin man in his eighties with a leonine head of thick, white, wavy hair, Wallis Newman was a gruff man who had a reputation for being terrifying with local politicians and dignitaries. Mary never understood that. Wallis reached up to pat her cheek, his fierce gaze softening into tenderness.

"Have a good time, kiddo. I won't wait up."

I want to stay home with you, Grampa, she thought. She glanced toward the hallway and sighed. Victor and Tim were waiting. She threw her arms around her grandfather's neck, hugged him swiftly, and left.

Now Victor pulled the car into a parking space, and Mary scrambled out thankfully. The parking-lot lamps washed the scene in harsh white illumination and sharp shadows. In the distance, she could see the warmer glow from flickering beach fires and the tiny pinpoints of colored lights strung in the trees and bushes that clustered around the lighthouse.

Tim bounced out happily. Victor locked the car and straightened, his movements slow and deliberate. Mary felt the skin around her eyes tighten as he glanced at her briefly. Then Tim loped around the car, planted a smacking kiss on her forehead so hard he almost knocked her over, and said, "I'm going to get in line for some food. Meet you on the beach?"

"All right," she sighed, and she forlornly watched him dash away. There goes my chaperon and bodyguard.

Victor curled a hand around her upper arm, and she looked up with a start, then tried to smile. The effort was not returned. "I want to talk to you," he said tersely.

As if on cue, the first round of fireworks exploded overhead with a rolling boom like thunder, and Victor's marble-carved features were washed in red and blue.

This was worse than a mistake, she thought, as she glanced again at the crowd on the beach. This was more like disastrous stupidity. There was no way they were going to run into Chance, and Victor was obviously upset, and she didn't have the energy to explain anything to him. Even if she'd known how to explain it.

Then a small seed of resentment bloomed. She shouldn't have to explain anything. They may have dated for a few years, but they hadn't even come to any kind of formal agreement. She never asked Victor what he did when she wasn't with him. Why was he suddenly treating her like his property?

"Now is not the time, Victor," she said firmly, and she gave him a no-nonsense nod meant to put him in his place.

Apparently he didn't get the point. His fingers pressed into her flesh as he said, "When will be the time to talk about it? Tim's gone for now—we have a few minuets. Who was that man I saw you with earlier? I heard you had dinner with him."

Mary blinked in surprise. Who'd told him that— Harold Schubert? Another member of the hospital staff? "So I had dinner with him," she said in an offhand manner. "I was eating—he was eating—we sat at the same table. It happens, Victor."

"But then you went out the door with him, and your car was still in the parking lot when I left. Did he take you home?"

Boom went another bout of fireworks. The crowd cheered. Mary fumbled for something reasonable and conciliatory to say, but what could that be? He'd taken her home and kissed her, and walked away with her soul in his pocket.

She scowled and said, "So what if he did? Is that a crime? He offered and I was too tired to drive, and anyway—why are you checking up on me like this?"

Suddenly his demeanor changed, became soothing. His grip on her arm loosened, and he rubbed her shoulders. "I'm sorry. That sounded bad, didn't it? I was just worried about you, darling, that's all. I didn't know him and thought you didn't, either, and if you'd wanted a ride home, all you had to do was ask me. I would have been happy to take you."

Mary's bristling smoothed over, and she turned contrite. Poor Victor. He'd had a long, hard day, too. "I knew your shift wasn't over until eight, and anyway, he was perfectly fine."

"So who was he anyway?" Victor asked casually, starting to lead her toward the beach.

"He teaches at the university. He was on Harold Schubert's yacht when the boating accident happened." And I can still feel his kiss on my mouth. The scorching memory engulfed her; with a shock, she felt the private area between her legs throb gently.

She looked around in confusion, cheeks flaming. She was too tired; the barrier between thought and action was too ephemeral, untrustworthy. She was afraid of what she might inadvertently blurt out if Victor continued his interrogation much longer.

Over the staccato explosions overhead and the noise of the crowd, she could hear the roar of an approaching motorcycle, and absentmindedly glanced in that direction.

The roar subsided into a low engine growl as a Harley-Davidson pulled into an empty parking space. There were two riders, a man driving and a woman riding pillion. They both wore black helmets and protective leather jackets. The man was wearing straight-legged, faded jeans and a white T-shirt, and the woman's lush, curved legs were bared by a black minidress. She wore, Mary saw with amazement, high-heeled stiletto pumps.

There was something familiar about the man's large, powerful body. She watched as he lowered the kickstand with the toe of his boot and they dismounted, removing their helmets.

The man's overlong blond hair lifted in the breeze. The woman's hair tumbled out, a long, curling, glorious mass of coppery red. They locked their helmets in the bike's carrier, chatting together companionably, and turned to the beach.

Mary's heart emitted one hard, dismayed kick. Chance, his tanned, chiseled features relaxed, the wide breadth of his shoulders a tough, aggressive angle in contrast to slim hips and lithe, muscular legs. The woman, the hourglass shape of her body extravagantly feminine, her leather jacket unzipped to reveal a deep neckline that showcased a lovely, generous cleavage, her long green eyes gleaming like a cat's.

Without realizing it, Mary had stopped dead in her tracks. She didn't notice Victor tugging on her arm, or that he'd turned to follow her gaze.

Now there, she thought bleakly, is a complete picture. It wasn't supposed to be a buxom blonde on Chance's arm after all. It was supposed to be a blazing, flamboyant, redheaded siren, with fingernails out to the next county and legs that would stop traffic. She glanced down at her own slender body, the coltish hips and legs, the even smaller waist and the slight, delicate curve of young breasts. And you're nothing to write home about, are you, Mary? Your outfit it pretty, but not eye-catchingly sexy. No. Actually, it's pretty forgettable.

I want to go home now and take the phone off the hook. I want to go to bed and pull the covers over my head and pretend this whole sorry day never happened.

"Oh look, Mary," said Victor cheerfully as he put an arm around her shoulders and pulled her close to his side. "There's your friend now. Let's go say hello."

"I want to go find Tim," she protested, wild to go anywhere, be anywhere but where she was. I don't want to go over there. I don't want to exchange pleasantries with him, try to pretend to be nice to her. I don't, I don't.

But it was too late. The couple by the motorcycle had seen them, too. After a long, narrow-eyed stare in their direction, Chance draped an arm around the redhead's shoulders, swept back her hair, and bent to murmur into her ear. The redhead looked their way, as well, pursed her lips, then smiled slowly.

Mary was swallowed by a surge of pure hatred.

The redhead slipped her arm around Chance's waist, and they strolled toward Victor and Mary. A few years younger than Chance but older than Mary, her body moved sensuously, a perfect complement to his catlike, prowling grace.

Am I getting sick? Mary wondered hopefully. Do I have to go home now?

Fireworks crashed. Green, everything turned green.

"Good evening," purred Chance as the couples converged. "It's Dr. Newman, and—let me guess. Victor?" His eyes, as he looked at the other man, glittered hard and dangerously bright.

Victor's arm tightened. "What a coincidence," he said smoothly. "We were just talking about you. I'm Dr. Victor Prentiss. You and Mary have met, I know."

Victor extended his free hand, which Chance appeared not to notice. Mary fixed her gaze somewhere in the vicinity of Chance's chest and remained silent.

The redhead took Victor's hand and shook it. Her voice was low and husky as she replied, "Nice to meet you, Doctor. I'm Cassie Grant, and of course this is Chance Armstrong." She drew back and eyed Mary curiously and with a hint of surprise. "So this is your new friend, Chance? She's such a sweet little thing."

Mary wanted to curl up and die. Sweet little thing. The words reverberated in the great big, lonely space inside her head. Her gaze, weighted with hot burning lead, fell to the ground.

Chance ran his hand up and down Cassie's arm and drawled insolently, "Isn't she? And she's a doctor, too. They work together, Cass. She and Victor make such a lovely, professional couple, don't they?"

Mary stiffened, feeling pain and surprise in equal measure, and her gaze flashed up. She took in

Chance's angry, wicked countenance, the other woman's thoughtful frown and Victor's sudden, creamy smile.

They were all so sophisticated, she thought bitterly, so sure of themselves with their social veneers and rapier cuts. She felt like a mouse surrounded by a gang of predatory alley cats.

The scene blurred. She muttered, "I'm going to find my brother," and before he could stop her, she slipped out from under Victor's grip and bolted.

There were four more rows of cars, then an open expanse of grass filled with spectators. Tim would be waiting in line at the vendors on the beach. She threaded her way quickly through the people.

A warm, hard hand curled around her arm again, and a shiver went down her spine as she turned around. A burst of white and red lit the sky like a demonic backdrop, outlining Chance's head and shoulders and throwing him into silhouette. Still with that hateful drawl in his voice, he said, "Running away, Dr. Mary? It was just getting good. Victor was about to throw down his white glove and challenge me to a duel."

She hated scenes. She tried everything she could to avoid them, but now, cornered, she rounded on him ferociously. "So why don't you go back and the three of you can get on with it? You've already got a heroine—fight over that redheaded witch and quit tormenting me!"

His hard white teeth gleamed in the shadows. It was hard to tell if he was smiling or snarling. He took her by the shoulders and pulled her close. She could smell leather and the faint, spicy tang of after-shave, and the corners of her mouth drooped with distress, even as her legs weakened with sexual awareness. The tremor ran up her body and seemed to communicate itself to him, for his hands gentled on her, the fingers sliding across her skin almost in a caress.

"Mary." The hard-bitten edge of nastiness had left his voice. "You're really upset."

He sounded so surprised, she thought. What had he expected I was doing—enjoying it? She crossed her arms around her middle and thought of Victor, and of Chance arriving with Cassie. "I'm having an awful time."

He reached up and smoothed back her hair. "I'm sorry. I didn't know you were coming with Victor."

"I didn't know you were coming with Cassie." That came out so miserably, she was ashamed of herself. When was she ever going to get that social veneer that other people had, so she could hide behind it when she needed to? His hand was warm, and lingered; she resisted the urge to turn and bury her face in his palm.

He hesitated, then said with a tone of self-disgust, "Cassie is my half sister, Mary. What's Victor to you, or haven't you made up your mind yet? He seems awfully possessive."

Half sister? Oh, but that meant— She played the scene over again in her mind, Chance catching sight of her and Victor, the intimate murmur to his companion, the arm around her shoulders. Suddenly the cloud of tears that had hovered over her head blew away, and Mary grew positively light-headed. She said dreamily, "We've dated for a couple of years. I—don't think I—care for him as much as I thought I did."

Her hands had risen of their own accord and settled lightly on his corded wrists. She could feel his pulse beating slow and strong under her fingertips.

"Oh. Have you told him that?" He cocked his head. Now, it was definitely a smile. "Or should I? I'd like that."

Heat burned her cheeks. If she kept blushing this way, nobody would have to tell Victor anything. "Oh, I . . ." Her voice trailed off breathlessly. I don't know what to do. My head keeps getting fuzzed up with other, more heady things. She heard herself say, "I like your after-shave."

He chuckled quietly, put his arms around her and drew her close against his broad chest, and tucked her head under his chin. She made an incoherent, questioning, absurdly happy sound. "It smells better up close," he murmured. "I didn't get the chance to tell you how pretty you look."

Somehow she had slipped inside the opening of his leather jacket, and his deep voice vibrated against her soft cheek. He was so large, so encompassing. He surrounded her with himself, and she nestled in the warm cave he had made of his body and marveled at the deep sense of contentment that stole over her. Her arms slipped around his waist and she leaned on him and sighed.

"You look good, too." He didn't, though. He looked bad in such an exotic, enticing way, he could make her forget all about good plain common sense. She didn't feel afraid, though she thought she ought to. She felt safe—protected. She wondered when reality would hit her.

Her loose, waist-length fall of hair spilled over his arm. He sank his fingers into it. "Your phone number's unlisted, Dr. Mary. You want to give it to me, or should I call you at work?"

She stared up at him, thrilled. Two and a half hours away from each other, and he'd tried to look her up. Her home phone number tumbled out of her mouth, and he repeated it, eyes gleaming with satisfaction.

Victor's frigid voice sliced into the warm cocoon where she was hiding. "Mary, are you all right?"

She jerked, startled, and Chance's hold tightened briefly before he let go of her and stepped back. The night breeze seemed chilled in contrast, and she touched her hair self-consciously as she summoned up a bewildered smile.

Victor stood with Cassie, his slim, elegant body taut and expression mildly inquiring. But his eyes were furious. She felt again that sinking sensation from earlier. Cassie, she noticed, was watching Chance closely, but his bland face showed nothing. "I'm— fine. How are you, Victor?"

He ignored that and strode up to interpose his body between her and Chance. "I thought you were going to look for Tim," he bit out.

Oh, Lord. Was she ever going to get a measure of control over what happened that evening? She looked around and was overwhelmed with relief to catch sight of Tim winding his way slowly through the crowd, laden down with hot dogs, elephant ears, cans of soda and bags of chips. "There he is!" she squeaked. "Hi, Timmy! I've been looking for you."

Tim glanced up with a wide grin, took in the scene of adults around him, caught sight of Cassie, and dropped a can of soda. His eyes rounded and grew lambent with love-struck awe. "Uh, I got some for everybody—I thought... Hi."

Mary put a hand to her forehead, which had begun to throb. What next?

Victor whispered tightly, "Mary, don't think this is over. You and I are still going to have that talk."

God, she owed him some kind of explanation, the way she'd been acting. She put a hand on his arm and murmured, "Later. We'll talk later, I promise."

Cassie said loudly, "Why don't we all just make it one big party and go find somewhere to sit down?"

Mary followed the rest of the group as they searched for an open space to settle on the beach. Chance shrugged out of his jacket and offered it to Mary to sit on, and then lounged back on the sand. Victor stationed himself on her other side like a guard dog. Tim passed around food, hovered around Cassie like a bee to a honey pot, and exclaimed over the fireworks. Cassie, who had removed her high-heeled shoes and carried them dangling from one hand, responded with friendly amusement to his incessant chatter.

Tim's making enough noise for all of us, Mary thought as she chewed without interest on her hot dog. Bless his heart. The unpredictable silence between the two men was gnawing at her stomach. Chance appeared to be relaxed enough, propped back on both elbows with legs crossed at booted ankles, but Victor was vibrating with hostility.

The food was sitting like rocks in her middle. She put half her hot dog down, uneaten, and glanced at Chance. His T-shirt glowed very white against the darker hue of his tan. He looked back at her, his eyes lit from the fire in the sky, and for one brief moment they glowed strangely feline.

Then his lips pursed quickly in a kiss. Her head snapped around and she stared at the shore in front of her. Then she sneaked a peek back at him. He winked. Incorrigible man! She whipped around to see if Victor had seen any of it.

He had. He was staring balefully at Chance, jaw out.

Mary set her drink down so hard, soda splashed out of the can.

I want to go home. Now. I mean it this time.

Cassie's low, husky voice said in her ear, "Hey, sugar, could you show me where the rest rooms are?"

"Yes," Mary moaned, and she shot to her feet.

"I could have shown you," Tim said brightly.

"Sorry, soldier. This trip is girls only. Come on, honey." Cassie took her hand and led her away.

Mary squeezed the older woman's slender fingers in a silent message of gratitude. Cassie squeezed back before letting her hand drop, then she lifted her red hair up and shook it out with a gusty snort.

"You might want your shoes," Mary suggested. "There might be broken glass around the rest rooms."

"That's all right. I don't really need to go. I just thought you might like to get away for a few minutes," Cassie said. "Lord, you could cut the air back there with a knife."

It was a pretty powerful turnaround of feeling, to go from pure hate to such a sense of appreciation in less than an hour. Mary smiled tentatively and was rewarded with an instant warm smile in return. "Thank you, I did need to be rescued. It's been a long day, and I'm a little out of my depth."

"Looks to me like anybody would be, with those two acting the way they are." Shrewd green eyes studied Mary, but it wasn't an unkind scrutiny.

She asked impulsively, "Are you really Chance's half sister?"

"Oh, so he confessed, did he?" Cassie laughed. "Yes, I am. We share a mother, and a—certain sense of humor. Are you really a doctor?"

Mary chuckled. "Yes. A resident, actually."

"Chance said he met you in the emergency room this afternoon."

So he had talked about her? Mary's step grew springy until she seemed to float. "What else did he say?"

Cassie's gaze danced. "He said he was throwing his weight around as usual, and you threw it back again. He had such a note of respect in his voice, I got intrigued, because Chance doesn't respect much. Way to be, sugar."

Mary's chuckle turned into an outright laugh. It bubbled infectiously in the air around them, aerated like champagne.

In an impulsive gesture, Cassie swung an arm around her shoulders and then turned serious. "Hey, I've really enjoyed hearing about you and meeting you. Would you like to call me sometime, and maybe we could get together and talk?"

Mary's eyes brightened. Underneath that worldly siren image was a really warm person whom she'd like to get to know. "Yes, I would."

"Great! I own a bookstore in town called The Crystal Dragon, and I live above it. The number's in the book, and you can call any time. It rings all over the place. Maybe you can come over for coffee and cheesecake. Do you like cheesecake?"

"I love it." And maybe not only would she acquire a new friend, but she could also find out more about Chance.

Cassie covered a yawn with the back of her hand, and Mary yawned, too. "We'd better get back," Cassie said, "and see if anybody's still alive."

Mary was fed up with the emotional roller coaster she'd been on all day. She looked back the way they'd come and said wistfully, "Do we have to?"

Cassie paused and then said wickedly, "Well, no. I could run you home on my bike. Chance can walk home from here. Course, without a jacket you'd freeze to death and get bugs all over your pretty top."

Mary giggled. So the motorcycle was Cassie's. Chance still drove it like a professional. "And poor Tim would have to go home with Victor. I mean—" that, as Cassie started to guffaw "—I mean, Victor's mood wouldn't improve, would it, and—and—"

"I know what you mean. Your brother's a sweetie. Come on, let's go rescue him now."

They wandered back to the men, where they found Tim and Chance deep in lively conversation. Victor was standing a few feet away and talking with a surgeon from the hospital.

Tim had jumped to his feet as soon as he laid eyes on them, almost pointing at Cassie like a retriever. Chance, looking around, straightened more slowly.

Cassie bent and scooped up her shoes. "It's past my bedtime, ladies and gents. We ought to be leaving now, Chance."

"But you have to stay for the finale," Tim exclaimed.

Mary went over to him and said quietly, "I'm sorry, Timmy, but I'm so tired my head is spinning. I need to go home now, too."

"Oh, but—" the boy protested.

"Tim." Chance spoke his name good-naturedly, and that was all he said, but Tim shut up immediately and shrugged in resignation.

"All right."

Mary stared at Tim in astonishment. That was it? He hardly ever gave in that gracefully. She and Cassie weren't the only big turnaround of the evening. Unless she missed her guess, there was a serious case of hero worship for Chance going in her little brother.

Chance picked up his jacket and slung it over one wide shoulder, then walked over to Mary. She clasped her hands together nervously, feeling the strangest, strongest desire to reach out to him with open arms.

He stroked the back of his fingers down the side of her face and gave her a private smile. "Call you tomorrow, Dr. Mary?" he said softly.

She glowed up at him; she couldn't help it. "All right."

She felt rather than heard it: his breath taken in quick. He opened his fingers and cupped her cheek, features sharpened and eyes gone heavy-lidded. "I won't call early. Pleasant dreams, babe."

"Good night," she breathed.

This time Tim wasn't staring at her in astonishment as Chance and Cassie left. He was staring after them, as well. God, she thought with the beginnings of self-disgust, he's as moonstruck as I am. Aren't we a pair?

Victor wasn't moonstruck, though. As it finally occurred to her to see if he'd finished his conversation, she turned to find him watching her, not with the open anger from earlier, but with something else on his face, something settled and severe and waiting.

CHAPTER FOUR

THE trip home was, like the trip to the lighthouse, conducted in silence.

Tim was stretched out in the back of the Volvo, sleepily humming. Victor drove fast with a sharp, pre-occupied frown, while Mary stared out her window at the moonlit bay and wondered if there was any way she could postpone talking with Victor until they had both had some sleep.

Her muscles were loose and shaky, all her joints seeming to come unglued at the thought of how nice and warm and soft her bed was going to feel. Besides, a skeptical part of her was saying, how do you know that in the morning you won't be waking up to the realization that this afternoon and evening were just one long hallucination?

Chance won't call! He might be nothing more than some intense, hitherto deeply buried wish fulfillment. Just some figment of your imagination, a product of your overworked brain from too many long, hard shifts at work and not enough fun. Oh, Mary, you'll say in the morning, wasn't that a silly way to behave, and what do you have to show for it? One upset boy-friend and an "I'll call you in the morning".

He won't call. Men like Chance never call ... or so I've heard! He was only fooling around with me be-cause his real date for the evening came down with chicken pox. He's going to go home and put my soul in a pickle jar, and stick me on a shelf with all the other souls he's snatched. A soul museum, that's what he's got. We'll spend our time getting to know each other, all us souls. We'll chat about how life used to be before Chance came along. After all, what else is there to do when you're in a pickle jar?

Victor switched off the car engine. With a start, Mary realized that they'd arrived home.

Tim struggled to a sitting position, his face cracking into a wide yawn. "I had fun tonight," he said cheerfully. "Thanks for letting me tag along, guys."

"Hmm? Oh, you're welcome, Tim," Victor said automatically. "Why don't you run along inside and let me say good-night to your sister?"

Mary sighed. The time of reckoning had come. She suppressed the cowardly desire to run into the house with her brother, and twisted in her seat to give Tim a smile. "Yes, you go on inside now."

Tim frowned. She could see the thought go over his face. First he caught her kissing one man that evening, and now she was going to kiss another. But thankfully, all he said was, "I'll go on to bed, then."

She said to him, "I won't be but a few minutes, sweetheart."

He leaned forward and kissed her. His eyes asked her if she knew what she was doing.

Her eyes said firmly, of course I do, and I am absolutely all right. But her heart said differently. What her heart said she kept to herself.

Then Tim slipped out of the car, ran up the porch steps, and disappeared into the house.

Mary turned to face Victor, who was staring out the windshield and tapping his fingers against the steering wheel. The silence stretched and grew too thin, until Mary cleared her throat and said quietly, "I don't know what to say, Vic."

"You're attracted to him." His voice was flat.

She stared out of the car, feeling an ache in her chest. Why was she feeling achy? She couldn't tell from Victor's tone of voice or from his face if he was even hurt. Maybe it was her pride that was aching. All of her feelings were right out there for everyone to see, and she felt naked. Why prevaricate?

"Yes," she said. "I'm sorry."

"You're sorry."

She moved jerkily. "Yes, I am, especially if it's hurt you. I—wasn't looking for this to happen, Vic. It just happened. I don't even know him, I just—" I just know when—if—he calls tomorrow, I need to see him again.

His head turned toward her, and he looked at her at last, sadly. "I know you don't know him. I'll bet you haven't even had the chance to think this through properly." His hand came out to cover hers. "Mary, sometimes people can't help whom they're attracted to. It's what you do about it that matters. I'm worried about you."

She blinked down at his hand. It was, like the rest of him, fine-boned and graceful. She remembered Chance's hands, wide, strong and calloused, and so gentle. She thrust the thought out of her mind.

Victor was being so kind and understanding. Somehow he had managed to put aside his jealousy and was just being her friend. She hadn't expected this. The tension eased out of her body, and she grasped his hand tightly.

I'm worried about me, too, she thought, but said reassuringly, "Try not to be. You know how careful I am."

He smiled at that, stroking her fingers. "Yes, you've always been cautious, normally. I've just never seen you behave the way you did this evening."

That's because I've never behaved that way before. She rubbed her face hard. "I'm all right."

Was that the truth, or was that what she wanted to be the truth?

Victor said gently, "Are you all right, darling? Don't underestimate Chance. I've heard a few things about him today that are pretty disturbing, from people who know him well. He's made conquests far more worldly and jaded than you are. Apparently he has quite an—appetite, and no respect for marriage vows."

The words slapped Mary in the face. She forced herself to breathe evenly; why was she so shocked? She'd already admitted, to herself and to Victor, that she didn't know anything about Chance.

But she was disappointed, crushingly so. There had been such a birth of hope in her today, she was only now beginning to conceive of how deep and far-reaching it had gone. Despite her innate caution, despite the glimpses she'd seen of his predatory sensuality, she'd focused instead on Chance's gentleness, the sense she had of being protected, even cherished. She'd even dared to hope that the erotic heat they had shared was something special and extraordinary for him, too. Instead it seemed that all her fears had been realized.

She could have nothing important in common with someone who didn't respect marriage vows. Even his own sister said he didn't respect much. And he'd come into the hospital with a married woman whose husband came in much later. Her husband couldn't have been on the yacht. Was Chance having an affair with her?

Welcome back to the real world, Mary.

Victor was watching her, his dark gaze attentive—was it pleased? Her shoulders bowed down. No wonder he didn't berate her with his jealousy. He'd had something far more substantial to say.

She said leadenly, "I've got to go in now, Vic."

"Yes," he said immediately, his voice soothing. "You need to go to bed. I need to get home, too. I'll call you?"

"Yes, all right." She stared at him as if he were a stranger. Charming, handsome, patient, safe Victor. If that was to be the definition of her life, why couldn't she find pleasure in it? Why couldn't she feel for Victor what she had felt for Chance?

Maybe that would come with time. Maybe someday soon she could look at Victor and be pleased with the thought of what their life could be like together. Maybe it was only because of what had happened today that she felt trapped. After Chance it all looked so sterile.

"How do you feel about having children someday?" she asked suddenly.

He froze in surprise, then smiled indulgently. "I think children might be wonderful, someday. When both our careers are going well, anything could happen."

"But that could be years for me. I'm twenty-six—what if I don't want to wait that long?" she persisted, feeling her eyes prickle.

His smile twisted, and his eyebrows drew together. "And throw out all your hard work? You're tired, darling. Everything will look better tomorrow."

"Will it?" she whispered.

"Of course it will." He leaned forward and pressed a kiss against her lips.

It was a light, undemanding pressure, warm and pleasant enough, but no fireworks. Mary dutifully kissed him back, and kept her eyes closed to hide how teary she was.

He pulled back, looking as smooth and unruffled as ever. "Good night, darling."

No "I'll walk you to your door", no gentility, no protectiveness, no romance. "Good night, Vic," she whispered.

She climbed out of the car, entered the house without looking back, and went disconsolately to bed.

Mary slept long and hard, and then a large, shadowed figure slid into her bed.

He was a familiar figure, that man, very much loved and desired. She murmured wordlessly and held her arms out to him, and he pulled her against his warm, naked body.

His wise, sensual fingertips woke her to a piercing pleasure. He whispered things in her ear, love words, promises. She clung to him, believing in the passion, the promise. He knew everything about her and cherished the knowledge, and spent his life protecting what they shared.

Just one thing bothered her. She couldn't remember what he looked like. She stroked the hair off his forehead, felt it slide silkenly between her fingers, and tried and tried to picture his face.

It was too dark to see his features. She reached to turn on the bedside lamp, but the light switch was broken. Then he kissed her hard and slid away.

She awoke, still aroused, her sweaty legs tangled in the bed sheets. Loneliness flooded her as she realized it had just been a dream.

A splinter of bright sunlight showed in the crack of her bedroom curtains. She rolled over to glance at her clock. It was almost three in the afternoon.

Mary curled into a miserable ball, a pillow tucked against her stomach. What was the matter with her? She'd never had such an erotic dream before, and certainly had never dreamed with such longing of a life partner.

Sure she wanted to get married. Sure she wanted children. But those had always been rather distant desires, something that she wanted to have someday, when she was older and ready for it, when she'd met the right man.

Then she would explore, with eagerness and faith, all the intimacies that a husband and wife shared, both the physical and emotional. Until then she would be content to wait, a chrysalis in a cocoon, for that first trembling emergence.

Tim had been five years old when their parents had died, and Mary had been just seventeen. The latter part of her teenage years—indeed, all through undergraduate school—had been devoted to being his surrogate mother.

She hadn't needed to take on such a demanding role. Their family was rich, and they could have afforded all kinds of quality child care. But she loved her brother deeply. She had wanted to do it. At a time when other young women were dating and exploring adult relationships, and often making disastrous mistakes, Mary had been either studying or watching Tim grow up, sharing with her grandfather Tim's childhood milestones.

She'd taught him how to ride a bike. She'd been there, cheering and waving a tearful goodbye on his first day of school. More than a brother, Tim was almost her son.

By the time things had settled enough for her to consider a little exploration of her own, Mary was in medical school and settled into the habit of a quiet life. She was able to judge for herself, calmly and rationally, the risks of casual sexual contact, and she had decided to wait for a serious, committed relationship. She had not achieved that level of commitment with anyone yet, not even with Victor.

And she had been content with that. Before, she had been content.

Now she said to herself starkly, I am a twenty-six-year-old spinster. Yes, a spinster. What an awful, sad, ridiculous word.

Maybe it was time to find out if Victor wanted to get engaged. Maybe they could get married next spring, have the wedding of the social season, spend their honeymoon in the Bahamas, come back home and—get back to work.

The prospect didn't sound any better today than it did yesterday. Feeling terribly sorry for herself, Mary buried her face into her pillow and snuffled. Marrying—well, anybody else was even harder to picture than marrying Victor.

That's it, she thought. In thirty years I'm going to be a skinny, shriveled-up old woman, with Coke-bottle glasses and gray hair, and Tim's children will call me Aunt Mary.

She gritted her teeth, rebelling against the fatalistic depression. Surely that's not it. Why I'll—I'll maybe take out a personal ad in the paper. "Wanted: a NICE, faithful husband and father type, not obsessed with careers or social climbing, must like Tim."

And picnics. And walks on the beach.

And having fun.

I'm not going to think of Chance. He's out of my life—not that he was really in it for long. I'm sad about Cassie, but if I called her and we became friends, sooner or later I'd run into that man. And I couldn't do that. No, a clean break would be best. That's it, it's over, shut the door on it and get on with things, kaput.

What if he calls today? He might, he just might. I can't lie in bed any longer—I've got to tell everybody I'm not home.

Mary surged out of bed, hurried to shower, and dressed in a Greenpeace T-shirt that said "Otter Joy" and shorts. Then, with her hair hanging loose and damp down her back, she hurried downstairs.

She told Tim, who was listening to music on his headphones in the study. She told her grandfather, who was stumping around in the back gardens with their handyman, plotting what he was going to tear down next year. She ran off to tell Janice, their housekeeper, who was busy vacuuming the front reception rooms. Only then did she relax enough to eat a sandwich, some freshly baked cookies and a glass of milk. She left the kitchen afterward, intent on finishing a book upstairs.

The hall phone rang just as she passed it. She picked up the receiver and said, "Hello?"

Damn!

"Hi, Mary." The voice was deep, growly and unmistakably Chance.

Shock bolted down her spine, and she panicked, slamming down the phone. She held the receiver down with both hands and stared at it as if it might jump off the hook and bite her. After a few seconds, it rang again. She jumped and looked around wildly. No, there was nobody else around.

"Janice?" she called weakly.

She could hear the rumble of the vacuum cleaner, and Janice singing loudly. The phone sounded again.

Don't—don't pick it up. Let the answering machine get it. She looked at the machine and whispered, "Tell him I'm not home."

The phone stopped ringing, and the machine played its message. She hovered, heart pounding idiotically, and then there was an electronic beep and Chance's voice sounded on the speaker.

"Mary? I know you're there, Mary. Are you okay?" A pause. He sounded so real, so vital, close enough to touch. He sounded both nettled and amused. His voice lowered confidentially. "This is Chance—is Victor there? Is that why you won't pick up the phone, Doc?"

Mary chewed her fingernails. The message time on the tape was thirty seconds, but it seemed to go on forever. Stop now. Stop. Then finally, thankfully, the machine clicked over, and she sagged. Her T-shirt clung to her clammy skin.

There, that was it. He had to have gotten the point. She didn't want to talk to him. It was over. She sniffed and blinked hard. "It" hadn't even started, and my, hadn't she been lucky?

The phone rang again. She shot away from it until she was pressed against the opposite wall. This time he sounded worried.

"Mary, if you're still there, please pick up. If you don't, I'm coming over—"

She lunged, snatched up the receiver and said breathlessly, "No, don't! Don't come over! That's all right—I'm fine! Everything's fine here now, and—and I have to leave the house for the whole day, so—that's it. Thanks for calling—"

"Wait a minute!" he interrupted sharply. "What's gotten into you? I told you I was going to call today—you gave me your number. What's going on, babe?"

Her hand shook badly. Her voice did, as well. "I've changed my mind, that's all. Please don't call again. I—I—I'm sorry, I just made a mistake yesterday. I was tired, I didn't know what I was doing—"

"Victor," he snarled. "What the hell did he say to you?" There was a faint, tight sound, as if he'd sucked in his breath. "I want to talk to you," he said more calmly. "I'm on my way."

"No—please—" The connection went dead.

He was on his way over. He was coming over here, oh, yes, because he knew where she lived, didn't he? Now what did she do? She would just have to tell him to his face—she would just have to look up into his face... Her hands fluttered frantically; her eyes darted around.

A cowardly part of her lifted up a finger. Or she could just run away.

Right! She'd told him she was leaving; he couldn't say she hadn't warned him. She raced up the stairs, grabbed her purse from her bedroom, fumbled for keys as she ran back down and out the door and toward her Cabriolet convertible that was parked in its usual . . .

No Cabriolet convertible. Not anywhere she looked. Oh, DAMN! It was still back in the DAMN hospital parking lot because he'd given her a ride home since she was too DAMN tired to drive herself!

She shook the fist that held her useless keys, spun around to stare at Janice's Toyota parked to one side, and spun back toward the house. Janice's keys. That's what she needed.

She froze then, hearing a sound that couldn't be happening. No, that's not a car coming up the drive. Her back hunched, and her shoulders crept around her ears. No, that had to be someone else. Nobody could get here that fast, call one moment and arrive the next.

Unless he had a car phone, Mary. Do you remember if he has a car phone, Mary?

She peeked over her shoulder, took one look at the black Jeep Cherokee that was pulling smoothly to a stop twenty feet away, squeaked and ran.

Into the house she streaked, flying past Tim up the stairs and into her room. She locked the door, panting, and leaned against it.

Other people could deal with Chance. Tim could.

Tim would tell Chance she wasn't home. Oh, God. She put her face in her hands.

Chance got out of the car, watching her disappear into the house like a frightened rabbit that's smelled a hawk. His tension eased a bit as soon as he had seen that she was all right, at least physically.

He removed his sunglasses and stretched himself, squinting at the door. Something certainly must have happened between last night and this afternoon; unless he had severely misjudged her, Mary was not the sort of woman to play stupid games. She really was spooked. He glanced at the Toyota parked beside the driveway and wondered if it was Victor's. No, he thought, smiling in spite of himself. Dr. Prentiss probably drove a Mercedes, or something equally impressive.

He debated for only a moment about whether to follow her or not, and then strode purposefully to the porch. Whatever Victor had told her, Chance was not about to concede without a battle.

He leaned on the doorbell until Tim answered. The boy was chewing pretzels from a bag in his hand. His grin, at least, was a welcoming sight. "Hi, Chance!"

"Hey, Tim," he said warmly. "Good to see you again. Can I come in?" Gain entry, that's the ticket, and then on to the next phase.

"Sure." Tim stepped back from the door. "You here to see Mary?"

Inside, Chance glanced around the spacious entry hall, heard the nearby whine of a vacuum and a deep female voice belting out show tunes. The decor was deceptively simple: a beautifully kept hardwood floor, tan rugs, cream-painted walls with dark wood trim. The effect was airy and homey.

He made his body relax into an easy, nonthreatening posture. "Yes, but I'm not sure she wants to see me," he confided, putting a hand on Tim's bony shoulder. "Did you have a good time last night?"

"Oh, sure, it was great! How's Cassie?" His eyes, large and clear sky blue like his sister's, were very bright.

Chance kept his face bland. "Just fine. I talked to her this morning and she said to tell you hi. Is Mary around?"

Tim appeared to deliberate. Chance kept his eyes steadily on the boy's gaze, waiting. Finally Tim shrugged. "She went up to her room. You want me to tell her you're here?"

He hesitated, looking past the foyer to the stairway. "Well, I guess she knows that. Tim, do you have any idea what happened last night after the fireworks? You rode home with Victor and her, right?"

"Yeah."

"Did they talk much?"

"Not on the ride home, but I went in as soon as we got here, and Mary came in later."

"I see." He angled his jaw out, realized how that must look, and drew a breath. "She didn't say anything to you today?"

"Only that I was supposed to say she wasn't home if anyone called."

Chance put his hands on his hips, thinking. What had happened in the car after Tim left? What did you get up to, you son of a ... Did you tell some lies, Dr. Prentiss? Or some carefully twisted half-truths you may have plucked from the rumor mill? Or—

The sudden, jarring thought seized up his brain. Maybe Victor had seen his perfect, rosy future slipping away, and gotten off his duff and proposed to her.

Oh, that would be rich, he thought bitterly. Victor realizes what a fool he's been, Mary realizes she really does care about him more than she thought, and they skip hand in hand to a swanky condo in the suburbs and throw gala parties for their prissy society friends. I'll be damned.

He felt Tim's eyes on him, and forced a smile. "Think she'd mind if I just went on up?"

"That's all right. I'll come down," said a very dignified voice from overhead. Tim and Chance both looked up. Mary stood ramrod straight at the top of the stairs. Her pale face was tense but composed, her eyes bleak. Her tawny hair was half-dried and floating around her narrow, delicate face in wavy tendrils, and her bare legs were slender as a gazelle's. Chance's gaze fell to her hand as she clutched the banister; the knuckles were white. She looked so vulnerable, his breath caught.

Mary was determined to follow through with the resolution she'd made in her room. She'd gotten herself into this mess; she should see her way through to getting out of it. Whatever Chance may or may not be, she was partly responsible for what had happened yesterday, and she owed him that much.

It was far from easy, though. Clad in olive green fatigue pants and a black mesh top that hid none of the tanned, powerful bulges of his broad chest and shoulders, he held his tough, muscular body warily, as if ready to spring up the stairs at the slightest provocation. His face was hardened, mouth grim, and his unblinking eyes, by some trick of the angled afternoon sun, looked slanted and tigerish, lit from within.

She gulped audibly. She had to go down and face that, and tell it she never wanted to see it again. The gulp turned to a scowl. What was it doing wanting to see her anyway? Couldn't it see that they were woefully mismatched? It needed to go pick on somebody its own size.

She marched down the stairs, nodded to her brother, who hovered curiously at the foot, and said, "We'll be in the sun-room, Timmy."

"Right," the boy said, backing up. "See you later, Chance?"

"You bet, son." Chance watched him go, ran his fingers through his hair, and pivoted back to Mary.

Wordlessly she led him to the back of the house. The sun-room was filled with plants, and finches twittered in large bamboo cages. A round white table and chairs were in the middle of the tiled floor, and screened windows were open to a fresh light breeze.

She felt, rather than heard him prowling along behind her. For such a large man, he moved silently.

She didn't stop moving until she was on the far side of the table. Then, hands twisted tightly together, she turned, half-expecting him to be right behind her.

But he had stopped and rested his hands on the back of a chair. Leaning on it, he looked at her expectantly from across the table. As she watched, the muscles of his upper arms flexed fluidly.

"I apologize," she said, laboring hard to breathe normally. The words tumbled out too fast. "I've behaved badly, and I should have talked to you on the phone, but I've had a lot on my mind and—and—it just didn't happen. It was nice meeting you yesterday, but I have to say goodbye now." She paused. His eyes had narrowed. "G-goodbye."

Another pause as he scrutinized her face. Then he straightened and demanded, "Why?"

He seemed so angry. Her eyes rounded and then she looked down at her tangled fingers.

"Oooh...I'm...sooo...busy." This was too hard. It was a fine, brave attempt, but she just couldn't come out and say that she'd heard he was a womanizer and a cheat, and she didn't want to be put in a pickle jar.

"You're not that busy," he said in a low, clipped voice. "Why are you running away from me? You were just fine when I left you last night."

Another, more poised woman might have said, so I've changed my mind. You're not my type. Get lost, soldier. Mary's head ducked farther down and she muttered to her fingers, "I don't want to be one of your conquests."

"One of my—" The harsh words were bitten off, and he gentled his tone. "I haven't had a 'conquest' since college. You've been hearing some rumors that just aren't true, Mary, and I think you've been hearing them from someone who has a vested interest in scaring you away from me." He waited until the words had sunk in sufficiently, then asked, "Am I right?"

Mary's brows drew together. Victor had been jealous, she knew that, but he'd been so concerned. She could hardly believe that he was capable of that kind of manipulation. Or would it even have to be manipulation? He only told her things she could check out herself, and if she'd heard those kind of rumors firsthand, she would have been concerned, too. Whatever Victor's motivation, whether they were true or not was an entirely different matter. "I don't know. Maybe. D-do you go out with married women?"

"For God's sake, is that what you heard?" He moved impatiently. "I sometimes go places with friends who happen to be married. Male and female. Have I had affairs with married women? No. Have some idiots spread the rumor that I have? Yes. That's all the fun some people get, although it's not my idea of fun. It causes too much hurt. Are you the kind of person that listens to that garbage?''

He sounded accusing, and he had every right to. Her shamed gaze traveled up to his grim countenance. "Not normally."

His expression eased. "Then why'd you listen this time? You had me really worried."

Her fingers flowed apart, and she reached out to the air between them. "I wish I hadn't listened. It made me feel awful about what happened yesterday, and I didn't want to feel that way about it. It's just—nobody like you has ever shown an interest in me before. I'm not your type, and I couldn't believe you were for real."

He walked around the table toward her with a lazy stride and a slow smile. "Now how would you know what my type is? What about you? Do you have a type?"

The tip of her tongue crept between her teeth as she smiled back and her shoulders started to climb toward her ears again.

His smile widened into a grin as he reached her, and he tucked a strand of hair behind her ear. "Everybody's got some idea of what they want. What kind of guys have you dated?"

She considered making up a whole portfolio of hopeful, dashing young suitors, and a small snicker exploded out of her nose. As if she could pull that off. "Victor."

He looked blank for a moment, then said, "You're kidding. That's it?"

She frowned uncertainly, and her cheeks heated. Was that a compliment? "Well, no. I really have been busy."

He cocked his head. "Too busy to date? No pretty young lady should be too busy to date."

"Oh, well, you see, there's Tim, and our parents died when I was seventeen, and I was in school an awfully long time, and I—well—" She bit down on her tongue hard. Don't tell him you're a virgin, blockhead! "I . . . don't care for the country club much."

"All those crisp, clean boys in their tennis whites, courting their Buffys and their Tiffanys, and talking about which boards of directors their fathers sit on," he said wryly. "No, I can't see it. Mary?"

"Hunh?" She smiled up at him tentatively.

"Promise me something?" The creases at the sides of his mouth deepened as she nodded. "Be careful not to get too caught up in Victor's point of view. I don't think he's looking out for your best interests right now. If you haven't got anybody to talk to, my sister Cassie said this morning that she's looking forward to your call. She's a smart lady, and she doesn't hesitate to call a fool a fool. Even me, when I'm acting like one. Which isn't often, by the way," he added with a twinkle.

She twinkled back delightedly, feeling not only warmed by his suggestion but pleased that Cassie had mentioned her again. Another thing she hadn't had time for was making friends. Most of the young women her age that she'd met in college couldn't identify with her parental-like concerns and life-style. She had a few friends at the hospital, but they were Victor's friends, too.

"I'm looking forward to seeing her, too. I liked her."

He ran a finger caressingly down the side of her cheek, and her stomach fluttered. "I've got a meeting tonight, but I'd like to take you out soon. When's your next free evening, Dr. Mary?"

Not for ages and ages, she thought with sudden gloom. Saturday was her next evening off, but she'd promised to go to dinner with Victor and some of his friends. Oh, bother, they were supposed to be going to the damn country club, too. Victor liked the country club, she remembered with a brief chill. What did that say about their compatibility?

"Saturday," she burst out. "I'm free Saturday." The trapped feeling from last night finally loosened and fell away, and she beamed up at him. "What do you want to do?"

His face softened and he stepped closer to her. She caught the faintest, tantalizing whiff of his after-shave, and her muscles went wobbly. "Have you been to the fair yet?"

"I usually take Timmy," she murmured huskily, "but this year I haven't had time to."

"Saturday's the last night. Would you like to go?"

Guilt and alarm flashed in her eyes. He was going to offer to take Tim, too, now. And if he wasn't, shouldn't she say something? She couldn't go and not take Tim. He'd never forgive her. "Yes, I love the fair. And maybe, would you mind, could we take Tim?"

"I was thinking of inviting Tim," he said smiling, "on maybe a different night. Just him and me. Don't you think he'd like that better than playing fifth wheel to us?"

"Oh, good Lord, yes. He'd love it. Are you sure it's no trouble?" She searched his face closely.

"Of course not. I'd enjoy it, too, otherwise I wouldn't have offered. I like Tim. I'll talk to him about tomorrow, and why don't I pick you up at six on Saturday?"

"That'd be wonderful." The glow was back; she could feel it radiating off her face in waves.

Chance took her face between his hands, tilting it up carefully. His hazel eyes were warm. "Don't get engaged in the meantime. Promise?"

"Promise," she breathed.

He bent and placed his mouth lightly over hers. Her eyes closed and she swayed against him, feeling again that tremendous rush of heat. Her hands splayed across his chest. His lips stroked hers languidly, while his long fingers cradled her skull as if it were fine china.

After a long, pulsing moment he pulled back from her trembling lips. She wore the expression of a young woman dreaming.

"I'd better go," he said hoarsely. "See you soon, sugar."

He had already left the sun-room before she could get her eyes unglued. Dazed she stared around her, heard Tim in the distance whooping with joy, and she dragged out a chair to sit down with a bump.

Sugar. Her lips curved softly. He'd called her sugar.

CHAPTER FIVE

MARY had to go to work on Wednesday at 7:00 a.m. Her morning at the emergency room was filled with a patient allergic to bee stings who had gone into anaphylactic shock, a woman who had spilled boiling water on her hand, a boy who had stepped on a fish hook, and an elderly man suffering from sunstroke.

She was preoccupied during the few moments she had to herself with the memory of Chance from the day before. He had seemed so sincere, so genuine, that all her defenses had come down. Still, caution troubled her. Was he what he claimed to be, or was there some truth after all to what Victor had said about him? And what about Victor—had he been looking out for her best interests, or had he been prompted to say what he did out of jealousy?

Now that she had come to know him a little better, her instinct was to trust Chance, but still she knew almost nothing about him, and what she did know was only what she'd heard from him. Victor, on the other hand, was someone she'd known for more than two years, and she'd grown to trust his advice.

Where was the truth? She didn't know, and she knew she couldn't begin to sort it out on her own. That was one of the reasons why she found herself calling Cassie at lunchtime. The other woman was delighted to hear from her, and they arranged to meet for brunch the next day at Cassie's place before Mary had to be back at work. She hung up after the conversation, pleased to have something to look forward to the next day.

Her feet had begun to hurt by two, and she was bogged down in the frenetic monotony of another endless day when Victor arrived at work. He came up beside her at the nurses' station when she was busy making notes on her latest patient. He put a hand on her back and smiled down at her warmly.

"Hi, Mary. How's your day gone?"

She straightened her shoulders with a sigh, pushed back her tawny bangs, and returned his smile. He looked sleek and fresh, but then he always managed to look classy, whereas she felt grubby and worn. "Oh, not bad, comparatively speaking. Mostly minor injuries so far today. You look nice. Have you had a good morning?"

"Yes, I played a few sets of tennis with Greg Aldrich. His wife says hello. They wanted to know when you and I could play doubles with them." He grimaced, still smiling. "I told them we'd let them know."

Mary withstood the temptation to make a face, as well. Victor was like a swan on the tennis court, a real pleasure to watch, whereas she was a fuzzy duckling, flapping and squawking after the balls with little hope of sending them where they were supposed to go.

She wondered if Chance played tennis. It somehow didn't seem like his type of game. What would he play for fun—pool?

That reminded her; she looked around quickly, but the E.R. was quiet. A woman was talking to Sandy at the front desk, and Julie was nearby making coffee. She lowered her voice. "By the way, about dinner on Saturday—I'm not going to be able to make it."

Victor frowned, his good humor fading. "Why not—what's happened?"

"Oh, something's come up, that's all." She bent her telltale face back over her notes and frowned thoughtfully. She really hoped he wouldn't press for details, because she didn't know what she would say. She was such a bad liar and knew it, and the truth right now would only start a conversation she didn't want to be having in front of Julie, or anybody else for that matter. Silently she urged him to shrug his shoulders and get on with other things.

"Something's come up? But I wanted to—" He bit back whatever he was going to say, looked around, as well, and took her by the arm. "Come on, let's go to the doctors' lounge."

"Oh, but..." Julie was watching them, bright-eyed with curiosity. Mary threw up her hands and went with Victor.

The comfortable, utilitarian lounge was empty. Mary wandered to the other end of the room as Victor closed the door and turned to her. He walked over slowly, smiling again, his dark eyes liquid.

He took her hands, rubbing his thumbs lightly across her palms. "Mary," he said tenderly, "I was going to ask you on Saturday, but if you can't make it, I'll just have to ask now."

She stared at his hands, at his face. Oh, Lord, she thought nervously, what now? He'd never acted like this at the hospital, and someone could walk in on them at any moment. "Victor, maybe we ought to have this—whatever this is—this conversation some other time, don't you think?"

"But our schedules are so busy, and I can't wait until next week." He raised her hands and pressed his lips against her fingers. "I think it's time we considered getting engaged."

She squinted at him tiredly. Engaged. He looked and sounded so sure that she was going to be thrilled, and dutifully she waited a moment to see if that would happen. A week ago it might have happened. Shouldn't she be feeling something right then, other than how sore her feet were? "Oh, Victor."

For a brief moment his eyes narrowed, then he stepped closer to put his arms around her. "What's the matter, darling—can it be that much of a shock? We've been dating for a long time, and we're so compatible. We have similar careers, we understand each other, and you've got to know how much you mean to me. Don't you think it's time to make some formal plans?"

She bowed her head and fiddled with a button on his white coat, troubled. There it was, the possibility to get everything she had been yearning for yesterday. A husband, a home of her own and a family someday. Commitment, security, a life mate. She heard herself saying, "But Vic—do you love me?"

His arms tightened. "Of course I love you—that's what I've been telling you. When I saw you hugging that man the other night, all I could think about was that you were mine, and he shouldn't be touching you. I want to make it official—to let everyone know that you're mine, and I'm yours. I mean, I certainly don't want to see anyone else." An edge crept into his voice. "Do you?"

She sagged and leaned her forehead against his chest. Now what do I say? she asked herself. I can't tell him about the pickle jars, or the real reason I canceled Saturday. I can't tell him that I can't get engaged because I promised Chance I wouldn't. Besides, I'm not sure I want the kind of life Victor does, and maybe that's why I'm not feeling anything like what I think I should be feeling.

He had put a hand at the back of her neck and was massaging her muscles. "Mary?"

"I—this is such a surprise. I wasn't expecting this. It's such a wonderful offer, but—I need to think about this, Vic." She looked up at him hopefully. "Give me some time?"

In the space of his hesitation, they heard his name called over the intercom. "Dammit," he said absently.

"You've got to go." She smoothed the coat over his chest. "Listen—give me the weekend to think about it, and we'll talk soon. I promise. That's not so much to ask—we've been careful every other step of the way."

His name sounded again, and Victor conceded with a sigh. "All right, darling." He bent and kissed her suddenly, hard. "I do love you."

She stroked his hair gently. "I love you, too."

Then he was gone to answer the summons, and left alone, Mary slapped a hand over her eyes. She was getting a first-class headache.

She did love him. She'd meant what she said. You don't choose to share so much of your life with someone without growing to care for them deeply.

But did she love him enough?

Cassie's bookstore, The Crystal Dragon, was located in an old restored house on Main Street near downtown. It was in an older, colorful neighborhood filled with small shops and residences, within sight of the lake. The lawns were dotted with oak and maple trees, and normally would be strewn with bright toys and bikes, but on Thursday the weather had turned chilly and a fine drizzle had started to fall. Mary had dressed accordingly, in faded jeans and a heather blue sweater, and before she entered the cluttered, spicy-smelling store, she patted the French braid that fell down her back to make sure it was still neat.

Cassie was wearing a green knit dress and a lot of sparkling jewelry. She greeted Mary with a bright smile, turned the Open sign to Closed and led her through the two spacious front rooms, which were the bookstore, back to a neat, well-appointed kitchen.

On the surface they didn't have much in common. Mary's life had been dedicated to Tim, school and medicine, whereas Cassie had left college to marry a career soldier, and had traveled all over the world. Upon the death of her husband seven years ago, she'd returned home to set up her own business. But however disparate their backgrounds, the warm rapport the two women had shared Monday was quickly re-established, and soon they were chatting over chicken crepes, salad and cheesecake like old friends.

Chance's memory was ever present. Mary saw him in the turn of Cassie's head, a gesture with her hand, the gentle affectionate way she had of calling her "sugar".

"Want another piece of cheesecake?" Cassie asked.

"Oh, no thanks. I couldn't eat another bite. Everything was delicious."

"My father—Chance's stepfather—is a chef. He and my mother run the Falcon Club. Do you know it?" Mary nodded. "He taught me everything I know about cooking. Didn't manage to teach Chance how to do much more than boil water, though.'' Cassie grinned. ''As a teenager, my brother was into other things besides cooking.''

Mary stirred cream into her coffee and stared into the rich brown liquid, thinking to herself, here we go. ''I'll bet.'' She took a deep breath and plunged. ''I've heard he's got something of a reputation.''

Cassie shifted in her chair and stroked one of her several cats, a calico that had come to settle in her lap. ''Yeah, I've heard the gossip, too. It's mostly based on conjecture and some things that happened twenty years ago. He used to be quite a rebel before he joined the army. This is a small town, and people's opinions don't change quickly. But even at his worst, Chance never really did anything that bad.''

Mary peered at her sideways. ''He was in the army? Did he join right out of high school?''

Cassie smiled a little. ''He didn't finish high school. He joined at seventeen, lied about his age—that used to be easier to do—and got an equivalency while he was in. It was a brief stint—Chance never did like taking orders. But something about the experience seemed to have focused him, because he went to journalism school afterward and there was never any question what kind of reporting he wanted to do.'' She smiled wryly. ''Name any place in the world that's been a war zone over the last ten years, and I'll guarantee you Chance's been there.''

Chance was a war correspondent. Mary fiddled with her spoon. She might have known. It fitted with her first impression of him as a dangerous, formidable man, and certainly explained why he traveled all over the world. Not a career academic at all.

"So—" she attempted to sound casual "—how old is he? He seems awfully young to have accomplished all that." A plump white Persian leapt up on Mary's knees, and she stroked its soft back gently.

"Unless he's lied to me, he's thirty-seven." Cassie chuckled, and Mary did, too. "And I doubt he could've lied to our mom. He's gotten all kinds of awards for his work. He seems to have a sixth sense for spotting trouble—apparently he can see the world as if it's one big chessboard, and anticipate everybody's moves. Don't ever let him talk you into a chess game for money, by the way." She rolled her eyes. Mary chuckled again, delighted at the wealth of information she was getting to feed her curiosity. "He took a summer teaching position to visit the family," Cassie went on, "but we're hoping to talk him into staying a while longer."

The teaching position wasn't permanent, then. He hadn't mentioned that. But from what he'd said in the car when he drove me home, he sounds at least ready to think about settling down. "So," Mary said offhandedly, as the cat stretched under her hand and purred, "does he date much?"

"You've been listening to those nasty rumors about married women," Cassie observed shrewdly.

"No," she said quickly, "no, oh, well—I've heard them. Yes. But hearing isn't the same as listening. But it does make one wonder if one should be listening." She winced. "If you know what I mean."

"It's all right. I know what you mean," Cassie assured her with a smile. "He's made some husbands jealous, and quite frankly left a few wives disappointed. That's how the rumors got going, but it's never been true. I'd know if it was—Chance and I don't have any secrets between us. He's one of my best friends.''

Mary's eyes and face brightened until they were glowing. I believe her, she thought. I wanted to believe him, and wasn't sure I should, but she's so straightforward and there's no reason for her to be anything but honest.... A weight, previously unnoticed, left her and she felt buoyant. She confessed shyly, ''I'm going out with him on Saturday.''

''To the fair. I know, he told me. And he had fun with Tim last night,'' she said with a twinkle.

''Oh, did he? That's good. I know Tim had a great time. He couldn't talk about anything else this morning.'' Thinking about Saturday and how she'd canceled with Victor made her eyes cloud over. She scooped a morsel of cheesecake from her plate onto her finger and let the cat lick it off. Chance said Cassie was a good person to talk to, and she was such a good listener. ''Cassie, we don't know each other very well yet, but may I confide in you about something?''

''Of course.'' The other woman's voice was kind.

It all spilled out in a tumbled rush. The two years with Victor, the two days with Chance, the passion, the perplexity, the proposal. Even the pickle jar came out. Wanting children and more fun in her life, and the choking feeling she had whenever she went to work. When she started to confess how guilty she'd felt canceling her date with Victor to go out with Chance, and how she'd put him off when he proposed to her, Cassie frowned.

''You've been dating Victor for two years,'' she said slowly, ''and he asked you to marry him yesterday?''

She had begun chewing a thumbnail. Was that disapproval she saw in Cassie's face? ''Yes,'' she said quietly. "But I didn't—I didn't accept. I just didn't tell him the whole truth yet."

Cassie tapped her fingers on the table, a thoughtful scowl on her face. "Well, my, my, my," she said after a moment. "There's something you ought to know, sugar. I don't think you're going to like it."

Mary started to feel terrible without knowing why. Was it something about Chance? Maybe he was deeply involved with somebody else, and Cassie thought she should know all the facts before she made a decision about Victor.

Cassie reached out to take her hand, looking steadily into her eyes. "I don't know how to put this delicately, so I'll just say it. Victor called me and we went out Tuesday night. I asked him how serious the two of you were, and he said not serious."

She wasn't sure she was hearing right. Her mind and body seemed to be encased in mud. "Not serious?" she echoed slowly.

"He even called this morning and asked if he could see me Saturday, for heaven's sake." Cassie's green eyes snapped. "I never got around to telling him Chance is my brother, and he didn't have a clue you and I would be talking. Why would he, after all the tensions on the Fourth?"

"But..." Slowly the mud boiled away, leaving behind incredulity, hurt, outrage. Victor had proposed to her. Victor was seeing Cassie, had every intention of continuing to see Cassie after he'd told her—how had he put it? That he certainly didn't want to see anyone else. Her hand spasmed tight on the cat, and startled, it meowed and sprang away. Two years of trust, a valued friendship—if they hadn't had anything else but that, she'd have thought surely at least they'd had that. Her breathing grew rapid, and her mouth trembled.

"I don't know what to say, Mary." Cassie was looking at her sadly. "I'm sorry."

"Oh, don't. It wasn't your fault." She rubbed her forehead. The anger was growing. "Cassie, may I use your phone?"

"Of course you can." The older woman stood and handed her a cordless phone. "Are you going to call him?"

"Yes, if you don't mind."

"I don't mind at all."

Mary watched her own shaking fingers dial. Victor had the early shift at the hospital. He would be smiling, joking with the nurses and the other doctors, soothing traumatized patients. She asked for him and waited, and one small, bewildered part of her mind asked, could there be a mistake? Some kind of horrible, twisted misunderstanding? Should I give him a chance to explain?

Then his smooth, cultured voice sounded in her ear, and she erupted. "You son of a bitch!" she hissed.

"What the hell—Mary?" Victor exclaimed.

She overrode him, spitting fury. "I know what you did, and I know what you were going to do! You and I are through. Don't you ever call me again, and as far as I'm concerned if you have anything to say to me at work, you better call me Dr. Newman!"

He spoke sharply. "God—Mary, what's got into you? I haven't done anything. What the hell are you talking about?"

"Whatever else I may or may not have done, I have never lied to you! Not ever! And I tr-trusted you to do the same for me!" She swiped at her burning eyes.

"And oh, by the way, Victor—my good friend Cassie Grant doesn't want to see you, either! She's right here, if you want to ask her for yourself!"

Dead silence. Then, "Mary?"

"What?" she cried. "What can you say, Victor?"

"I can explain—"

"Oh, save it for your next fiancée!" she snapped, and slammed down the phone.

Dead silence in Cassie's kitchen, as well.

"Well," Mary said, "I feel better." Then she burst into tears, and was turned, then pulled into a pair of welcoming, cradling arms.

She didn't have any poise or pride left. She buried her face in Cassie's neck and sobbed it all out. Cassie rocked her and stroked her hot face, and when the storm finally ended, she said, "There, sugar. Why don't you go wash your face and I'll put on some tea? Doesn't that sound nice?"

She nodded, sniffing, but then she caught sight of the clock over the refrigerator, and her face crumpled again as she felt her stomach bottom out. "Oh, God— I'm supposed to be at work in forty-five minutes, and Victor's there—"

"You don't have to go in today," Cassie said quietly. "It's really too much to expect from yourself, Mary."

After a moment she nodded. Then she called the hospital again, told them she wouldn't be coming in, and as Cassie made tea, she went upstairs to the comfortable, tiled bathroom to wash her face and pull the shattered pieces of herself together.

She could hear Cassie speaking on the phone. Not wanting to think about who she might be talking to, Mary wandered through the rest of the second story.

A large bedroom, obviously Cassie's, a smaller guest room, the living room facing the street. It was cheerful and had a fireplace, and was filled with plants and patchwork pillows and bright prints with a fantasy theme.

Exhausted, Mary curled up on the large couch with a heavy sigh. She should call home and let them know where she was. She would, in a minute. She closed her sore eyes and fell asleep.

Muffled voices woke her up. A woman's and a man's. She looked around fuzzily, not knowing where she was for a moment. Then she remembered, and she dropped her head into her hands.

Don't think about Victor, Mary. He's not worth it. You don't have to face him until tomorrow, and by then you'll have figured out how to face him.

She pictured telling Tim and her grandfather about him and mentally cringed. Well. She didn't have to face that just yet, either.

The woman speaking was Cassie.

The man was Chance.

Chance? Her gaze darted around, fell on a clock on the mantel, which said half past four. She'd slept for over two hours. What was Chance doing here?

She touched her puffy cheeks and eyelids gingerly and patted her braid. It was crooked, and tendrils of hair had slipped out. She struggled to her feet, tiptoed to the bathroom, and stared at the horror in the mirror. Eyes swollen and red-rimmed, skin splotchy, hair like a scarecrow's—she wanted to crawl into the bathtub and pull the shower curtain.

Maybe Chance had just stopped by to borrow something. Maybe he would go away in a few minutes and she would only have to face Cassie. Facing Cassie was all right; the other woman had already seen her pride as dented as it could get. Hurriedly she shook out the rest of the braid and brushed her hair. Then she listened at the bathroom door. She couldn't hear anything. Maybe that meant he'd gone.

She opened the door and tiptoed out, head ducked, and bumped into someone's chest. It was a very large chest, and male, covered with a butter-soft, fawn-colored chamois shirt and smelling of a familiar, sensual after-shave. Her shoulders hunched, and her head ducked farther. The ground never opened up when she wanted it to.

"I happen to be going home now," she whispered without looking up. "Excuse me, please."

He folded his arms around her snugly, and something like a croon rumbled from his chest to her. "Cassie told me what happened. I'm sorry you got hurt, Mary."

He said it so gently, tears pricked her eyes. She balled her hands into fists and shuddered. "I'm not going to cry anymore, dammit," she gritted. Somehow her face got plastered into his chest. "And don't you look at me."

A pause. He fitted a hand to the back of her head and stroked her hair. "I have my eyes closed now."

"Promise?" The sharp chill of the pain was easing as his body warmth seeped into her.

"Promise." He pressed his mouth to the top of her head. "Can you bear to hear my opinion?"

"What?" Her arms crept around his waist, and she rested against him. He shifted slightly, planting his legs farther apart to take her weight.

"He wasn't right for you. Even if he'd been what he seemed to be. He's not your... type." He rubbed his cheek against her hair.

She rubbed her cheek against his soft shirt and, incredibly, found herself smiling. "How do you know what my type is?"

"I know."

"So what is my type?" She inhaled deeply, such a private pleasure, and took his scent inside.

"Someone who takes you out to play, who wants to father your children, who would rather see you walk away from your career if it doesn't make you happy," he said quietly. "Someone who likes your finches, and your brother, and who doesn't give a damn if you're stinking rich or dirt poor. And someone who thinks you're beautiful even when your face is all splotchy from crying, although he'd want to do everything he could to keep you from crying." He paused thoughtfully. "Someone who doesn't like the country club. Yes, I think I've got it."

He was reading her like a road map. How had he gotten to know her so quickly and so well? By the time he had finished speaking, Mary had tilted back her face to stare up at him, wide-eyed.

Looking at him while he spoke was almost like looking into a puddle of water. She could see the image he created, but she was afraid to reach out and touch it, for fear that it would break into ripples and disappear.

"You paint a pretty seductive picture," she said unsteadily.

"You painted it, Mary." He traced the delicate skin under her eyes. "I'm only telling you what I see. And there was no place in that picture for Victor, was there?''

"No."

His eyes crinkled at her. Soul-stealer's eyes; she could see herself, tiny and unblinking, overlaid on the rich hazel. "No. Although I don't approve of his methods, I can't blame the guy for trying to fit into it. Just don't cry over him any more, all right?''

She smiled, and it was a gentle, more serene beginning. "All right.''

He kissed her on the forehead. It was such a simple, chaste caress she felt vaguely disappointed, but also grateful that she wouldn't have to cope with more right now. "Cassie's taken a great many liberties, I'm afraid. She not only called me, but she also called your home and told your grandfather you were over here. And she's cooking dinner. So it's all arranged. You've got to stay now or you'll disappoint her, and she'll ruin my evening.''

She chuckled. "I wouldn't dream of doing that. I better go down and see if I can help.''

"It stopped raining while you were asleep, so I'm to grill the hamburgers. Do you like beer?'' Still talking, he slipped an arm around her shoulders and walked with her down the stairs.

Cassie was chopping eggs, and the kitchen was filled with the homey smell of baking bread. There was an apple pie ready for the oven on the counter. She looked up as Chance and Mary appeared and blew a strand of curling red hair out of her eyes.

"There you are," she said comfortably as Chance went out back to light the charcoal. "Want to tear up some spinach for the salad? What do you think—baked potatoes or French fries?''

''French fries, please,'' Mary said happily, and got to work.

CHAPTER SIX

MARY'S grandfather was livid the next morning when she told him about Victor. Very much gratified, she paused to collect her thoughts so that she could approach telling Tim in a much more careful fashion. After all, Victor had been a part of Mary's life for a long time, and so, in a smaller way, a part of Tim's. She omitted the details about Cassie and told Tim that she and Victor had reached a point where they had to decide whether they would continue to see each other or not, and they had decided not to.

Tim, who had been fixing the gears of his bike in the garage, straightened slowly and asked, "Are you all right, Mary?"

Her insides melted. He sounded so adult, so concerned. She hugged him tightly and said, "I'm fine, really. It's all over, and that's kind of sad, but in a way it's good, too. Are you all right?"

He looked surprised. "Sure, why wouldn't I be? I never liked him all that much anyway. He wasn't right for you, you know."

Mary closed her eyes, feeling a deep chagrin. Did everybody see that but me? She left her brother to his tinkering and went inside to get ready for work.

Her initial reluctance about going to work had turned into an outright dread. But no matter how she felt about it, the E.R. was as much her territory as it was Victor's, and she hadn't done anything wrong. She didn't have to speak to him except professionally, and after she'd calmed down enough to think about it, she suspected that he wouldn't try to speak to her. Victor wouldn't want to face the possibility of a nasty private scene at the hospital. It wouldn't look good. People would talk.

She marched into the hospital that afternoon, reassured the nurses that she was feeling much better now, and plunged into work. As she had thought, Victor avoided her, and while she didn't enjoy the long hours any more than she usually did, it could have been much worse.

Her relief came in at seven on Saturday, but she had to stay another hour to help with a traffic accident. When she got home, she ate breakfast, showered, and fell into bed at nine. No time to herself, no time to reflect, to think things over properly, to spend time with Tim. Something had to change.

She slept like the dead until her radio alarm went off at five o'clock. Mary rolled onto her back and stared at the ceiling, while the late-afternoon sun streamed across her bed and the disc jockey on the radio promised good weather for the rest of the weekend.

Good weather, she thought fuzzily. Her mouth felt like it was stuffed full of dry cotton. That's supposed to mean something.

"... and it's the last night of the county fair, folks, so get on out there and enjoy!" crowed the radio.

The fair. Chance. Six o'clock. Oh, God! She only had an hour to get ready. She leapt out of bed and raced toward her bathroom.

She dressed sensibly in jeans and sneakers, a bright red paisley sleeveless top with a scalloped neckline and a matching bow at the nape of the neck. Some red lipstick and she was ready.

Forty-five minutes later she was wandering restlessly around the first floor pretending to find small tasks to occupy herself with. She straightened the already-neat books on three shelves in the library, carefully inspected all the plants in the sun-room—Janice always kept them well, and they were in fine shape, but gardening was another thing she missed having time for—and was alphabetizing the spices in the kitchen when the doorbell rang.

She raced for the door, collided with Tim in the front hall, and abruptly realized what she was doing. "Go on, get the door," she told her bewildered brother, and pivoted to run into the study, where her grandfather was watching a movie on PBS. "Hi, Grampa," she said breathlessly as she skidded to a stop and perched on the arm of his chair.

Chance and Tim were talking in the hall. Wallis squinted up at Mary with a frown. "Done inspecting the house?" he said gruffly.

Her cheeks pinkened. Footsteps approached. "What're you watching?"

"Not gonna answer, huh?" he muttered. "I want to meet this young man who's got Tim so talkative and you so flustered."

"I'm not flustered. Don't you dare say that to anybody," she hissed in his ear as Chance and Tim appeared in the doorway. She changed the whisper into a kiss on the cheek. Wallis grunted with laughter, patting her hand, and they both turned to the new arrival.

Chance had a companionable arm draped around Tim's shoulders. He was dressed in tight, faded jeans, as well, with a forest green shirt rolled up at the sleeves. The color brought out the burnished gold of his hair and deepened the richness of his tan.

His gaze winged to her immediately, and he smiled slowly. He was so lazily, prowlingly sexy the breath whoofed out of her in a silent rush as she smiled back.

Tim was laughing at something he'd said. Wallis gripped the arm of his chair, eyes glittering, and barked out, "So, young man. You want to take my granddaughter out tonight, do you? What have you got to say for yourself?"

Mary's head snapped around and she stared at her grandfather in surprise. He'd never acted so bristly with Victor. What had gotten into him? "Grampa!"

Wallis looked at her unrepentantly. "What?"

A dancing light had entered Chance's eyes. Suddenly he looked devilish, unpredictable. He drawled, "Why, I say that I'm looking forward to having a good time tonight. Hi, Mary. You look great. Nice to meet you, Mr. Newman. I've heard good things about you."

"Hmph! I've heard things about you, too." Wallis's eyes narrowed, and he said pointedly, "Harold Schubert and I had quite a conversation the other night. Can't say I like everything he told me."

Oh, God, Mary thought worriedly, Grampa's heard the rumors. This could turn ugly.

Chance appeared to be unaffected by the cross fire, however, as his arm dropped away from Tim and he strode composedly across the room to stand beside the chair, almost as if he were offering himself for inspection. "Dean Schubert's a good administrator and one hell of a politician, but we both know it's part of his job to talk whichever way the wind's blowing,'' he said with an easy smile. "And certain influential people don't want me to be seen in a favorable light lately. I'm very glad that Mary has the good sense not to listen to idle gossip, and find out things for herself. I respect that, don't you? After all, appearances can be deceiving.''

"Hmm. You have a point there, son." Wallis's bristling had died down, but he was still frowning. Tim stood to one side, watching everything in fascination. "I also heard from Schubert how you were quite the hero on his yacht Monday."

"I just did what needed to be done," Chance replied with a hint of discomfort. He glanced at Mary and rested a hand on her shoulder. Her bare skin shivered at his touch, and he stroked her gently with a light, subtle caress that only they were aware of. He seemed to come to some decision then, and said to Wallis, "Look, Mr. Newman. I appreciate your protectiveness, and I share it to some extent. But Mary's done a pretty good job of looking after herself so far, and will continue to make her own choices whether you and I like it or not. I can promise you, though, that I won't be doing anything against her wishes."

After a moment of considering that, Wallis conceded with a sigh. Mary took Chance's hand, stood and smiled down at the old man. "Don't worry so much, Grampa," she said gently. "I'm looking forward to tonight. I'll tell you all about it in the morning."

"It's my job to worry," grumbled Wallis, but his eyes had softened when he looked at her. "Go on now, you two, skedaddle. I'm missing my movie."

"Good night," Tim said brightly.

Mary gave him a quick hug. "Good night, Timmy. I'll bring you some caramel corn."

"See you later, Tim." Chance curled an arm around her shoulders and nodded down to Wallis. "Glad to meet you. Maybe we can talk more again sometime." His gaze fell on Wallis's chessboard on a corner table and he paused. "Perhaps over a game of chess?"

Wallis's eyes lit up. "Oh, do you play?"

"A little," Chance said offhandedly, the devil back in his eyes.

Mary recalled Cassie's warning on Thursday and covered her mouth to hide a grin. Who was the prey, and who was the piranha here? Don't, don't say anything. Leave them to work out their own footing.

Wallis invited him for dinner next week, and then Chance and Mary escaped into the sunny warm evening.

When they were outside, Mary glanced up at him. He still had his arm around her, and his lithe body brushed against her side as they walked. "I'm sorry about that," she said. "Grampa can be very old-fashioned sometimes."

Chance gave her a quick smile. "Don't apologize. I like him. If I'm ever lucky enough to have children and grandchildren, I'll be the same way."

He wanted children. Mary hugged that knowledge to herself and examined it carefully. She could just imagine what kind of a father Chance would be: gentle but firm, nurturing, protective, those square, capable hands cradling a newborn baby. She sucked in a breath, amazed and rather disturbed at the strength of the ravenous hunger that gripped her.

Chance opened the passenger door and helped her up into the Jeep. Mary watched as he rounded the front of the car, running his fingers through his hair in that familiar, habitual gesture.

They pulled onto the highway, Chance resting a hand on top of the steering wheel. The dark, concealing sunglasses highlighted the precision of his chiseled features, the clean angle of his jaw, the carved mobility of that wide, sensual mouth.

He glanced at her. "If you want, we can roll up the windows and I'll put the air-conditioning on. It'd help keep that floppy, pretty thing in your hair."

She felt as pleased as if he'd paid her an extravagant compliment. "No, it's all right. I enjoy the fresh air."

"You look good in red. You should wear it more often."

I will, she almost said. And bit her tongue. And thanked him demurely. She was starting to get worried about how ridiculously uncontrolled her impulses had become regarding him. It was another thing to think about when she had time. She was normally such a levelheaded, calm person. Or was that because her life had been so predictable and ordered before now? Maybe she was more tempestuous than she realized. Certainly she felt more alive than she ever had.

Chance laid a hand on her knee. "I meant to ask—how did work go yesterday? Did Dr. Pretense make a stink?"

Dr.... She started to laugh in surprise. "No, we pretty much avoided each other. It was uncomfortable, but not as bad as it could have been, I guess. It's rather hard to tell how things will be in the long run."

"And it doesn't exactly enhance a job you're already uncertain about," he added.

"Well, no." She sighed. "Still, I don't have to think about that until three o'clock tomorrow."

"Let's make a rule," he suggested. "No talking about work at all tonight, starting now."

"At least not about my work." She smiled. "I'd love to hear more about what you do, though. Cassie said that you were a war reporter."

They had reached the highway that led to the fairgrounds, where traffic was slow and heavy. He took his hand from her knee to downshift. "I wouldn't call it that, a war reporter. I write a syndicated column on international affairs, and write about peacetime as much as I do war. It's just that a lot of it involves military action. And a lot of travel, of course."

Mary hadn't heard of him before, but she didn't really keep up on whose name was on the bylines when she had time to read the paper. "Cassie worries about you. She said your family was hoping to convince you to settle down."

"Getting back in touch with family is why I've taken a nice, tame teaching job this summer. I may just hang around Cherry Bay until something else comes up." He must have sensed her troubled reaction because he gave her a reassuring smile. "The university has offered me a permanent teaching position, so who knows? Maybe I'll take it. I haven't decided yet."

She stared out the window, her brows drawn together. Visiting family was a good temporary lure, but Cassie had said that he'd won awards for his work. He must be highly regarded and very dedicated to his job. And settling down was harder than it first seemed to someone who was used to life on the road. "You must keep a close eye on the news." Did he ever see exciting things happen and wish he were there?

He lifted one shoulder and let it fall. "It's what I know. Mostly I'm a teacher now, with nothing more serious on my mind than whether or not I want to try writing that book I always meant to write."

She dragged herself out of her preoccupation and asked, "What sort of a journalism class do you teach?"

"It's called Government-Press Relations. How to talk to generals, senators, ambassadors, receptionists—you know, annoy powerful people who really wish you'd just go away." He grinned. "I've become very good at that."

She stared at the look of amused nostalgia on his face. Annoying powerful people, good grief! She drew a breath, again seeing the fascinating, alien species in him, and wondering how much they could really have in common. Mary didn't like to annoy anybody if she could help it. "Have you been in any conflicts?" She winced again. He would have had to have been, wouldn't he?

"A few." The grin was fading. "The military doesn't like the press to get too close, and once we've ignored their advice and come in anyway, we're on our own. They don't have time to baby-sit. Most people want to talk to the press, though. The really famous tragedies involving journalists, like hostage situations and executions, are pretty rare." His mouth twisted wryly. "It's not quite a walk in the park, but most of the time it's just a job."

He made it sound so easy. She knew he had to be glossing over some things. Had he ever been wounded, maybe lost friends? He must have been friends with Cassie's husband, who'd been in the military. When he'd driven her home the day they'd met, he'd said that he'd lost touch with his friends, and everybody he knew was a work contact. What an alienating job. And what if something blew up half a world away? Was he going to leave again?

The words fell out of her mouth. "Have you ever been hurt?"

He hesitated. "Once. Not badly."

"What happened?"

"I was in Belfast. A car bomb went off and I caught some glass in my shoulder from a nearby window."

She stared out the window again and confessed, "It sounds terrifying."

His fingertips brushed her cheek, and she jerked in startlement, turning to face him. For a moment she saw him in an entirely different light—a hard-faced, enigmatic stranger with shielded eyes and impenetrable thoughts. Then he took off his sunglasses and crinkled his eyes at her, and her vision realigned itself until she was looking at Chance again.

"It was a long time ago," he said quietly. "And I don't like that worried look on your face."

She smoothed her expression over quickly. "I'm not worried."

"Good, there's no reason to be. I'm a teacher for now," he said firmly. "And the only terror in that is what I inflict on my students, if they try to slide by without doing their work."

She chuckled. "Now that sounds terrifying."

"You better believe it. I'm their worst nightmare. There are rumors to that effect on campus, and trust me, all of those are true."

Mary knew from her student days that the university was one of the worst gossip mills in town. She could just imagine all the other rumors that would have circulated about such a good-looking, sexy, eligible man. The university was probably where all the gossip about him had started.

The fair rides had been in sight over the tree line for several minutes now. They finally reached the turnoff where traffic controllers motioned for the cars to park in lines set up in nearby fields.

Mary hopped to the ground and stretched while Chance came up beside her and took her hand. They went through the front entrance line, bought wristbands for unlimited rides, and paused just inside the gate.

The fair was noisy, crowded, dirty and very colorful. Mary looked around excitedly. So much to do, so little time.

Chance was watching her, the corners of his mouth quirking in amusement. So what; she didn't care. She inhaled deeply of the delicious smells coming from the food booths.

"Ladies' choice. What do you want to do?" he asked. "Eat something, go on a few rides, try to win Timmy a stuffed tarantula? There're the farm exhibits, too."

"I want to do everything, but could we eat first?" Hungrily she read the signs advertising shaved-steak sandwiches, Polish sausage, corn dogs, cotton candy, candied apples, lemonade... "I'm starving—I haven't eaten since I got home this morning."

His eyebrows rose. "Somebody needs to feed you more regularly. Between work and sleep, you're not getting your three squares a day."

She grinned at him self-consciously. "I have a high metabolism, too. I can keep up with Tim, and he's fourteen."

He laughed. "I can believe it. Come on, let's eat supper. Just don't complain when we hit the roller coaster."

She trotted to keep up with him. "Did I mention a cast-iron stomach as well?"

"Maybe I should worry about myself. It wouldn't be too genteel to be sick all over your shoes, would it?"

They bought Polish sausages on kaiser rolls, cheddar fries, candied apples and sodas, and went to sit at a nearby picnic table. While they ate the spicy meal, Mary was overly conscious of how his hard, denim-clad thigh pressed against hers, and how he turned to her when he spoke. He was finished before she was and propped one hand behind her on the picnic bench, leaning over her. He was making a cave of himself around her again, and she had no doubt that it was very deliberate. The teasing, flirting light from earlier that week was back in his eyes, and the constant awareness of him was a febrile tension that underscored everything she said or did.

She finished her apple and licked her sticky fingers slowly, eyes sparkling. Was he trying to seduce her? And was he succeeding?

I find you attractive, he said with every glance and brush of his body, with his instant responsiveness to her moods.

And she found that she felt attractive in a way that Victor had never managed to make her feel. When she gestured as she talked, and every time she moved her body, she was aware of herself as a desirable young woman in the presence of an extremely sexy man. It was heady stuff, and it went to her head like an exotic wine.

They walked through the farm exhibits next. Mary liked the horses best and so they lingered, petting the soft, inquiring noses of the curious ones. There was a small gray donkey in one stall with his nose in a far corner and his back to the passersby. His long ears were laid back against his head and he looked so disgusted, she had to laugh.

"Poor fellow, it looks like he's had enough and wants to go home."

Chance leaned one shoulder against a post and regarded the donkey. "Reminds me of a bad-tempered mule we had when I was a kid. He ate everything. Tennis balls, my mom's sandal once, a piece of my father's shirt whenever he could get his teeth into him. Everything except his feed, that is." He pursed his lips. "I tried to ride him once. No uppity mule was going to get the better of me. I've still got the scars."

"Oh, no, what happened?" she said, chuckling.

He shrugged. "We had a contest of wills, and the better man won. But then, I was only six."

She moved closer to him and leaned on the waist-high rail. "Did you live on a farm?"

"Yes, until my father left." His gaze went distant, as if he were seeing a different time and other things. "Mom tried to keep it going for a couple of months, but we had to leave." He focused on her again. "My uncle owns it now. Maybe I'll take you there sometime."

"I'd like that," she said quietly. "What happened to your father?"

"I don't know." The reply was terse, but after a moment he leaned his elbows on the rail beside her and continued, "We haven't heard anything from him since he left when I was seven. He could be dead for all I know. Or married with another family, which would be strange—having brothers and sisters you've never met, I mean. Anyway, I didn't miss out. We moved into town, and Mom met my stepfather, and he and I got to be close. It took some time. I guess I was pretty stubborn about it.''

Blond hair dripping into sad eyes, wanting their father to come home to them. It wasn't Chance's children after all; it was him. She could just see him. Behind the sadness would have been a fiery independence, the iron conviction of never trusting like that again. Mary ached gently for the ghost of the little boy, and she put her hand on his back, rubbing softly.

"Who wouldn't be?" she murmured.

He glanced at her ironically. "Yeah, but I was cutting off my own nose, you know? My stepdad's the best thing that ever happened to us. He came after me every time I ran away, and only really raised his voice the time I stole Cassie and took her, too."

"Oh, my..." A hand crept to her mouth. "How old was she?"

"She'd just turned four. I was eleven, and had just realized that I knew everything." One corner of his mouth curled up. "It was all right—I thought. I mean, she'd wanted to come. I did ask her. As I recall, she'd gotten in trouble for something or other that day, I don't remember what. Whatever it was, I'm sure she deserved it. Cassie was a hell-child, too. But at the time, we thought we'd go look for greener pastures. The police picked us up about two miles from home, which was just as well. The novelty had worn off for her by that point, and she had sat down at the side of the road and was refusing to walk any farther."

She could laugh, even if in horror; after all, the story had a good conclusion. "Your poor parents."

"Yeah, those were the good old days. It got worse." He reached into the stall, picked up a piece of straw, and twirled it between his fingers. "My mom's hair used to be as red as Cassie's. Now it's going white. I started aging her, and Cassie finished her off. And Dad never has lost that bewildered expression he had when I was a teenager."

She enjoyed the feel of his strong muscles under her fingertips, the graceful curve of his spine, the wide, rippling indentations under the green cloth as she worked over to one shoulder. She said uncertainly, "Surely you couldn't have been that bad."

He snorted. "You think. I've been through a couple of wars that were easier than my teens. Well, nobody would want to live through their teenage years again, would they?"

"I don't know," she mused, an edge of sadness shading her voice as she thought of her own high school years. In many ways it would be hard to relive them, but it had been a much simpler time—and her parents had been alive. "I could be tempted."

He turned, put an arm around her, and pulled her close against his side. "You really need to slow down, Mary. Enjoy things again. You don't have to be a kid to do that. Just stop living up to everybody else's expectations."

She cuddled into him and put her head on his shoulder. "Maybe. I am thinking about things. And I guess I don't really want to be a teenager again. You talking about your parents just made me think of mine. I still miss them."

"Does Tim remember them?"

"Not really. Just vague, blurred memories. I've told him a lot about them, though." She tried to steer the conversation away from such unhappy reminiscences as she said, "Tim's been fairly quiet so far, but in some ways he's young for his age. I keep waiting for him to explode into the Great Rebellion. Maybe you could tell me what I should watch for."

Chance smiled at her. "I'd be really surprised if Tim gave you the kind of trouble I gave my parents. He's such a sensible boy."

She couldn't resist asking, "What kind of things did you do?"

"Oh, mostly the usual. Ran with the wrong crowd. Drinking, smoking—I stayed away from drugs because I didn't like feeling out of control. I got arrested once for being in a stolen car, but I didn't know it was stolen and wasn't driving, so I was never charged." He glanced sidelong at her, and under his casual veneer was something more searching, an unspoken question.

She pressed closer to him, her expression nonjudgmental, just listening. He continued, "And I dated a lot of girls. Ran after anything in a skirt, really. This one girl—" He stopped momentarily, and the skin around his eyes tightened. "I got pretty serious with this one girl. We thought we were being careful, but she ended up pregnant." He drew a breath. "I was going to marry her, but her parents took her out of state for an abortion. I wasn't told about it until afterward."

He fell silent. In its corner, the donkey nibbled at a pile of hay. A couple passed by, chatting together. Mary was oblivious to it all, tracing in her mind's eye the path of his pain and disappointment, and how it had shaped him. That must have been when he enlisted in the army to get away from home. She reached up and smoothed the hair away from his forehead. "I'm sorry, Chance."

He turned to kiss her palm. "Things got better. She and I corresponded for a while, but after a few months that stopped. I did all right for myself, and she's still in the area. She's married now and has a family of her own, and we've managed to retain a friendship. In fact, she's one of those married women I'm supposed to be having an affair with. But her husband and I get along, too. He knows better."

"I'm glad you felt like you could tell me," she said huskily.

He straightened from the railing. "You made it easy, Mary. I didn't mean to go on so much, but you're a very good listener." Palpably, he shook off the mood that had settled on him and said, "Now that you know the worst of it, do you still want to sit by me on the roller coaster?"

"Of course I do."

His face lightened with pleasure and a relief he was far too proud to put into words. He took her hand, threading his fingers through hers, and they left the horse barn.

It was fully dark now, and the lights on the fair rides were a kaleidoscope of whirling color. The crowd was noisier and older, most of the parents with children having gone home at sundown. Loud music blared from speakers at the fastest rides.

Chance kept her close and smoothly negotiated a path through the crowd. A burly man, involved in a heated argument with his companion, nearly walked into Mary. Instead, he walked into an iron barrier as Chance shot out his arm protectively.

"Hey, why don't you watch where the hell—" the man began, and then saw Chance's face. "Hah. 'Scuse me." He and his friend dodged away.

Mary was hardly aware of the altercation before it was all over. She looked in the direction the man went, then up at Chance again. The fleeting hint of the hard-faced stranger was already gone before she was ever fully sure it was there.

"Which ride first?" he asked easily.

She smiled, tucked her hand into the crook of his arm, and they got in line for the Octopus.

Six rides later, they stepped off the Himalaya, a mini roller coaster that went very fast, both forward and backward. Mary was wobbling giddily, laughing at the look on Chance's face as he stared at her.

"Iron stomach is right," he said, laughing, as well. "Is there anything that you won't go on?"

"If so, I haven't found it. Tim and I spent the weekend at Cedar Point one time. I love the Demon Drop and the Blue Streak."

He raised his eyebrows. "Are you ready for more?"

"Sure."

They got in line for the Ferris wheel and stepped into their carriage when their turn came. The attendant put the safety bar down, and after all the other passengers got on, the wheel smoothly started to turn.

The breeze, over the tree line, was fresh and invigoratingly cool. It tugged at Mary's hair and blew long strands across Chance's arm and shoulder as she craned to stare, enchanted, at all the fair lights and the surrounding countryside. In the distance she could just see the lake, glimmering in the moonlight.

As they rounded the top of the wheel and began another descent, Chance put his arm around her and pulled her close. She turned to him with a smile. She caught a glimpse of his shadowed face before he put his mouth to her ear and said, "Do you know what's supposed to happen on the Ferris wheel?"

"What?"

His lips brushed the sensitive hairs at her temple. "You're supposed to share a kiss. Would you share a kiss with me, Mary?"

A shiver trickled down her spine and spread to her limbs. Their carriage swung back up again and ascended to the top. Her eyes drifted closed as she breathed, "Oh, yes."

His mouth was already covering hers. His lips caressed her delicately, over and over, shaping and rediscovering definition of taste. Her shudder deepened, and then he held the back of her head, parted her lips and delved in hard.

A moan broke from one of them; they shared the sound and drank it into silence. Then he crushed her to his chest and kissed her hotly. Time fell away, and the world spun gracefully. There was a rhythm to what he did as he bent her over his arm and pierced her repeatedly with his tongue. Each time, she throbbed with a spasmodic, agonized pleasure that was hunger.

He cupped the small curve of her breast with one hand, and her nipple hardened instantly into a small, round pebble. He sucked in a breath, rotating his thumb over the sensitive nub until she writhed mindlessly, needing to get closer, to reach for something she only understood instinctively.

He was shaking. She gripped the back of his head, murmuring incoherently.

The carriage stopped, and someone cleared his throat. "Hey," said the attendant, "you want to ride again?"

Chance lifted his head. Mary's face was naked, her wide eyes blind. He groaned, tucked her face into his neck and cradled her. "Let's get out of here, precious."

CHAPTER SEVEN

LEAVING the fair was a blur for Mary. Everything but Chance, who kept an arm protectively around her, was peripheral. His body was taut. When she looked up into his face, she could see a muscle bunched in the straight, clean line of his jaw, and she had to work hard to keep from stumbling.

It was close to midnight when they climbed into his Jeep and he pulled out of the parking space. The tension between them was unbearable, like atmospheric pressure just before a storm. He shifted, then put his hand on her thigh, stroking up the slender length of it. The sensation burned through the denim. She covered his hand with hers and swallowed dryly.

"Chance," she said hoarsely, "we have to talk."

He shot her an unsmiling glance, his hazel eyes smoky. "Yes, I know. Where do you want to go? Can we talk at your house? I could take you to mine if you like."

His house would be filled with his presence, and very private. What would it look like? She pushed aside longing, fought for caution and said, "I think we'd better go back to mine tonight. If you don't mind."

He inclined his head in a terse nod, his fingers tightening on her leg before he let go and turned his attention to the road. She leaned back against the headrest and looked out the window, absorbed in the rhythm of her racing pulse.

116

She had only understood in the most intellectual sense the passions that drove some people to disaster. Now, sharp as a knife edge, sexual excitement surrounded her, and all of her previously held convictions were terribly fragile in the force of it. His smallest actions, the rustle of clothing, the quiet sound of his breathing, caught and tugged at her. He was so beautiful he made her ache, and she was gripped with a fierce, primeval desire.

They pulled into the driveway, the tires of the Jeep crunching on gravel. He turned off the ignition, tightened his fingers on the steering wheel, then came around to open her door.

Mary couldn't look at him, even as she reached out and gripped his hands hard. She stared at the house instead. The only illumination that showed downstairs came from the front hall light and the porch light. The upstairs floor was dark. Grampa and Tim would be in bed, but it was such a large house that muffled sound that this wasn't any more safe than his place would have been.

She noticed a dark car, pulled to one side. It was a Volvo, and as she watched, the driver's door opened and Victor climbed out.

"Oh, no," she whispered. Chance turned sharply to follow her shocked gaze.

Victor strolled toward them, dressed in an elegant navy blue suit. His tie was loosened, white shirt unbuttoned at the throat, and his eyes glittered like black diamonds.

"Goddammit," Chance growled tightly. He moved fluidly to place himself between her and Victor.

Victor looked at him and his handsome face twisted. "I might have known it," he drawled. "You've been panting after her like a dog in rut."

Chance stood at his ease, feet planted apart, but Mary saw his fingers flex, a tiny, violent movement, and her heart started to hammer sickeningly. "Mary," he said quietly, "do you want to speak to Victor right now?"

"No," she choked out. "Victor, are you drunk? Go home." But no matter how offensive he was, she couldn't let him drink and drive—maybe she should call him a cab. . . .

Victor sneered. "That would be convenient for you. I spent two years of my life on you, Mary—and you threw it away like garbage. You didn't even listen when I told you I could explain. No, you had to believe that lying redheaded bitch."

Chance stiffened and took a step toward him, the broad angle of his shoulders menacing. "Mary, get in the house."

"No!" she said sharply, walking up behind Chance to put a hand on his rigid back. "Not unless you come inside with me. You should be ashamed of yourself, Victor! I'm embarrassed for you—"

"Embarrassed for me!" He laughed furiously. "What about all the times I was embarrassed to be seen with you! To think I coaxed you along, putting up with your social ignorance and tight-assed prudish morals. You're a misfit cartoon, Mary, and no amount of money or your family name will change that."

She recoiled as if she'd been slapped. Chance snarled and sprang forward, his body blurring, and suddenly Victor grimaced in pain as Chance pinned his arms behind his back.

Chance's features were contorted with rage, but his voice was still low and controlled as he clipped out, "He's not drunk, Mary, he's just a son of a bitch, a social climber who got knocked off his rung." He looked at her, and his eyes softened slightly. "Go on inside, sugar. I'll persuade Dr. Pretense to leave quietly."

Her hands twisted together. She looked at him numbly and nodded. "All right."

Chance force-marched Victor to the Volvo while Mary hurried up the porch steps. She paused, hand on the doorknob, looking over her shoulder.

Chance opened the driver's door and let go of Victor, who swiveled to throw a punch at his face. Almost casually, Chance's powerful body swung into a graceful maneuver, dodging the blow easily and knocking Victor's legs out from under him. The other man fell with a heavy thump and scrambled to his feet, cursing.

Chance said with what sounded like amusement, "Try not to be such an idiot. I'm not a doctor and you're not a fighter. You're outclassed, fool. Go home before you get hurt."

Victor stood stiffly, hands fisted. Chance leaned closer and said something to him in a low voice. Even from that distance Mary could see the other man pale. Then he turned abruptly, got into his car and sped away.

Chance pivoted, saw Mary frozen on the doorstep, eyes like saucers, and he quickly strode over to her. She said in a very small voice, "I never thought he would act like that. I never really knew him at all."

"Forget about him, Mary," he said gently, pulling her into his arms. Now that it was all over, she started to shake. "Don't look like that, sugar. He won't be back."

She buried her face in his chest. "But I wouldn't have thought he'd come here at all. What else is he capable of? He turned *violent*—he knows where Tim goes to school."

Chance rubbed her back, murmuring, "Ssh, now. This was a last-ditch attempt to get you back, I think, and when he saw me here his temper blew. He won't try anything else. I promise."

"But how do you know?" she queried anxiously.

His arms tightened and he said in a hard voice, "Because I told him what I would do to him if he did. He got the point. I can be a mean bastard when something I care about is threatened, and he not only hurt you badly, he insulted Cassie." He nuzzled her hair and she could feel him smile. "Nobody slams my sister except me."

But Mary couldn't laugh yet. She felt furious pain for what Victor had said about her, and another wave of outrage for Cassie's sake.

Chance said softly, "Let's go inside, precious. I could use a drink, and I think you could, too."

She hugged him swiftly and they went into the house. He followed Mary to the kitchen, leaning back against a counter as she asked without looking up, "Would you like a soft drink, or we have wine and brandy?"

"No beer?" he asked.

She smiled a little at that, glancing sideways. "No, sorry." She made a mental note to ask Janice to pick some up next week. "But the wine's good."

"That sounds fine."

There wasn't any in the fridge, so she pulled a bottle of dry French white from the rack on the wall and looked for a corkscrew in the drawer.

"Here," he said, "let me open that while you get the glasses."

She handed it over to him, went to the counter and got two wineglasses from the cupboard. Tight-assed, prudish morals, he'd said. Absently she reached for a chocolate chip cookie from the jar nearby and munched on it. A misfit cartoon.

Chance popped the cork while he watched Mary eat four cookies broodingly. He poured wine into the two glasses, then reached for a cookie himself. "You know," he remarked, "I can tell you're thinking about what Victor said outside."

Mary looked at him guiltily.

He suppressed a smile. Her face was so easy to read. "I know he said some hurtful things, but don't grant them any validity. He meant them to hurt."

She sighed. "I know. There was just enough accuracy in it to make it sting all the more."

He finished his cookie, then reached out smoothly to pick her up and set her on the counter, bringing her gaze more on a level with his. He planted his hands on either side of her hips and came nose-to-nose with her. "Mary Newman," he said sternly, "you are a gorgeous, refreshingly honest young woman. It's a compliment that Victor sees you as a misfit—who'd want to fit in with him?"

Her eyes stated to brighten. She'd begun to squirrel away all of the things he'd said to her: "sugar", "precious", and now, "gorgeous", to be pulled out and marveled over in private. She fiddled with a button on his shirt and admitted, "You have a point."

He raised a hand and laid the palm against her cheek. "And I don't think you're a prude. Not at all. Ever since I bumped into you on Monday, I haven't been able to get you out of my mind. For God's sake, Mary, I'm almost thirty-eight years old, I've been all over the world, and I was on that Ferris wheel this evening acting like a lovesick teenager."

Face flaming, her gaze dropped to the button she was playing with. It fell open and she caught a glimpse of the dark brown skin underneath, dusted with gold hairs. She snatched her hand back quickly.

"There's something I wanted to tell you," she said in a low voice. "I've not—I've never..." Her breath shuddered in her throat. "You see, Victor called me a prude for a reason."

Silence. His hand dropped to her shoulder and gripped her hard. "Never?" he whispered. "Not even with Victor?"

Mutely she shook her head, then peered up to see his expression. His eyes were wide, wondering. Of all the things she'd been afraid to see in his face, she'd never expected to see such vulnerability. Impulsively she cupped his lean cheeks and said unsteadily, "I never wanted to before. It was always easier to be safe, to say I'd wait until I had some kind of commitment. But now I'm so attracted to you I can't see straight. I'm not even prepared—"

He moaned and bent forward to kiss her, his mouth already open. She met him halfway, feverishly wrapping her arms around his neck, and he thrust his hips between her legs and crushed her torso against his. She sighed, arching against him. He bit her lower lip, one hand splayed at her lower back as he slowly, roughly ground his pelvis hard against her.

Pure animal need bolted through her. She was overheated, ravenous. She raked her fingernails across his back, and he yanked up the jersey material of her top to cup her breast. She didn't have on a bra and he inhaled sharply as he connected with bare, soft flesh.

She needed—she needed something more. She needed him. She sank her hands into his hair as he gently flicked her sensitized, erect nipple and ran his tongue down the side of her neck.

He stilled, gasping as if he'd run for miles. She burrowed closer, legs wrapped around his hips. He buried his face in her neck, grabbing hold of her waist as he groaned, "No—no, baby. Stop—be still now. Stop."

She sobbed out a whimper. His hold on her tightened to the point of pain.

"I know—baby, I know, but it's been years—" A violent shiver racked through him and he said raggedly, "I'm not prepared either—and if you do that sexy little wiggle with your hips again, I swear I might lay you down on the floor and take you right here and now." She froze, feeling his heartbeat thud against her chest in great, rapid strokes. After a moment his arms loosened somewhat and he sighed, "And that's not how it should be, precious. Not your first time. Your first time should be slow and tender. I want you to feel safe with me."

"I love you," she heard herself say, and caught up with it a moment later. Panic washed over her. As soon as she'd said it, she realized it was true, but she hadn't thought it through and had no idea what his reaction would be. Isn't that just typical, she thought with horror. No brakes between brain and mouth, everything I'm feeling and thinking right out there for anyone to see. She hid her terrified face in his shirt.

One large hand came up, trembling slightly, to caress the back of her head. He took several deep, even breaths. "Precious Mary," he whispered, enfolding her as he bowed to brush his lips against her temple. A pause. "I'm very much in love with you."

Tears sprang to her eyes, and she pulled back to search his face frantically. Had she heard that right? His expression was somber, still razor-edged with arousal, and his eyes were stripped. "My goodness, you mean it," she blurted out.

His face creased in a smile. "Of course I mean it. I love the way you can't hide anything you're thinking, and how much family means to you. I love the way you light up with pleasure at the simplest things, and your enjoyment at the fair. I loved watching you pet the horses, and how I could open up to you, and I even love the storm clouds and how bossy you can be."

"Bossy," she murmured, even as a sunburst of joy streamed through her. "I'm not bossy."

"You are, too, when you're feeling self-confident enough. You can't fool me, Mary—I can see right through you, and I love your pretty little bones." He brushed the hair off her forehead, turning intense. "And I especially love your innocence. I'm glad you've never been with anyone else. You belong with me."

She quickly turned to nuzzle his hand, whispering, "I love everything about you. I think I did from the very first day. I just couldn't believe that it could happen that quickly and still be something that would last."

"We can make it last," he said huskily. "Marry me."

She sighed and closed her eyes, resting her cheek in his palm. "Okay."

His hand jerked spasmodically. Then he muttered, "You'd better mean that."

"I do—I know it's awfully soon, but we'll be careful—we'll make sure it's right." She whispered, "I trust you."

He kissed her hard, a long, luscious, sensual mixture of tenderness and desire, and then he growled, "I want to make you pregnant. I want you to quit that damn job, and marry me, and have my baby. I want to watch you sleeping in the morning, with your hair spread over my pillow."

She groaned, loving the images he painted, running her hands greedily over his chest. "I want it, too."

He shuddered. "Dammit, we've got to stop this. I can just see Tim or your grandfather wandering down here for a midnight snack." He pulled back and gripped her hands. "Listen to me, baby. We've got time. I want you to think about this. I know you're saying that this is what you want, too, but you'd be giving up a lot—and I have to know that you're sure. If you marry me, it's forever. I won't let you go again. Do you understand?"

I am sure, she almost said. But something in his taut posture made her stop. "You're right," she said gently. For his sake, she would think about it, even though she knew her answer wasn't going to change. "We have time."

He pressed a kiss to her fingers. "I'll call you. And don't hang up this time. If you do, I won't be responsible for my actions." One corner of his mouth crooked up. "Talk to you tomorrow." He turned and left quickly.

Mary sat for a while on the kitchen counter, staring at the floor while her head whirled madly. She noticed the two full glasses of wine, picked one up and drained it, then drank the other. Two proposals in one week. She hiccuped. And a fistfight. She squinted. Well, almost.

It hadn't happened. None of it had. Her alarm clock was going to go off in a minute, and she would be late for work. She pressed her fingers against her lips, which still throbbed, and hiccuped again. Not quite the same as pinching. She fell off the counter, lurched over to the phone, and dialed. The desk nurse at the E.R. answered, and Mary demanded, "Am I late for work?"

"Dr. Newman?"

"Y-yes. Is this Paula?"

"Yes, are you all right?"

"I'm—" Hic! "—fine. How are you? Am I late?"

A rustle of paper. "No, Doctor. You're due in at three tomorrow afternoon." The nurse's voice had turned amused. "Have a good time."

"Thank you," Mary slurred with dignity. "I shall. Good night."

She replaced the receiver slowly and hung on to it. That settled one question: she wasn't late. But was she dreaming? She pinched herself hard and winced. Ow! It was real; everything that had happened that night was real. Chance was in love with her; she was in love with him. They were going to get married and have babies and spend the rest of their lives together.

Her eyes grew heavy-lidded, and one hand came up to cup her own breast. He'd held her there so exquisitely, and he'd pressed against the cradle between her legs as if he'd come home.

She left the kitchen to waltz serenely up the stairs to her bedroom. Things weren't exactly settled between them; as long as he'd asked her to think about things, there would always be that question in his eyes, something vital he held back from her. So she would think about things.

And what did she think about things? Why, she thought things were fine. She thought she'd never seen such a pretty bedroom like hers, and she was sure she'd never felt so wonderful in her life. She felt loved and desirable and wanted. She felt . . . beautiful.

She still didn't know much about him.

That was all right. They could get to know each other better while they were engaged. Already she felt she could instinctively predict so much about him. He would have a horrible temper when roused, and it would be a frightening sight if he ever lost control. But even in his worst temper, he would be careful, would take care. Protectiveness was imbued in every part of him; he couldn't do anything else.

But he wanted her to quit her job. Shouldn't she be more concerned about that?

I didn't like it anyway, she told herself happily, as with languid, dreamy movements she stripped off her dirty clothing and floated into her bathroom. I had all but decided to quit on my own, for reasons that have nothing to do with how I feel about Chance. And besides, even if I quit now, it'll just give me more time to decide what it is I really want to do. If I want to do anything besides keep house and look after our children.

Our children.

I want to make you pregnant.

The memory of how he had said those powerful words rippled through her, causing another gush of heated desire. She leaned against the tiled wall as the warm water from her shower washed away the dirt from the fair.

He and Tim got along so well, and after just one meeting, her grandfather had already begun to soften toward him. It seemed so perfect—wasn't it possible that everything would come together in one miraculous moment of epiphany, where she could look around at all the definitions in her life and see the pattern of her future as it was meant to be?

Mary believed it was. After all her caution, after all the adult years of holding back, of doubt and waiting, finally she believed.

She shook herself alert, stepped out of the shower, toweled dry, and quickly brushed her teeth. She had to hurry and go to bed. She had a lot to do in the morning. She had to call Cassie, type her resignation for the hospital, and be ready for Chance when he called. She had to decide the best method for being ready.

She climbed into bed, still so excited she was convinced she'd never go to sleep, and fell effortlessly into a darkness as soft as feathers.

Chance didn't call the next morning.

Mary typed and retyped her resignation on the personal computer in the study. A good night's sleep hadn't shifted her conviction that the residency just wasn't right for her. Finally she settled on a draft that she felt comfortable with, printed it out, and signed her name to it with a flourish.

Tim asked her curiously how her evening with Chance had gone. Wonderful, she sang, as she cooked him and her grandfather breakfast. Janice didn't come in on Sundays, and Mary loved to cook for her family when she had the time. Soon she would have much more time on her hands for all the things she loved and all the people she loved to do them with.

Wallis harrumphed grumpily and looked worried. It didn't stop him from polishing off five large pancakes and several strips of bacon, however, though he did make a few comments about how his eldest grandchild and cosseted baby girl was dancing and singing and carrying on. She patted his cheek affectionately and told them she was quitting her job at the hospital.

That was enough of a bombshell to divert their attention. After answering their many questions and concerns, she was both shaken and pleased to find how relieved Wallis was, while Tim was frankly ecstatic.

"Been having a few doubts of my own about you slaving away your youth," her grandfather told her.

"I know, Grampa," she said with a sigh. A thought had occurred to her: would she have listened to her doubts earlier, and quit while she was still in medical school if she hadn't listened too much to Victor? She put that aside for now; what was done was done. "It would have been different if I'd had more sense of a vocation, but I don't. Maybe I will someday. Or— maybe I'll look into qualifications for setting up a day-care center. I think I'd really enjoy that."

"You know you don't have to do anything if you don't want to," he said for perhaps the thousandth time. "I've always just wanted what would make you happy."

"We'll see. There's time." And she drifted into the kitchen, humming, to help Tim with the dishes.

She still didn't hear from Chance by noon. Lunchtime came and went. She called Cassie, and they had a long, involved, heart-to-heart about marriage and the future. Cassie promised to come over for lunch the next week, and Mary hung up after the talk more convinced than ever that not only was she ready for the engagement with Chance, but that she and Cassie were also going to be the best of friends. Then she went into the study to read some of her medical textbooks. She made a few decisions about just what she wanted and planned to stop at the hospital pharmacy sometime that day.

There was still no word from Chance by the time she had to get ready for work. She found his number in the phone book and dialed it, but all she got was a busy signal. At two o'clock Mary was starting to droop. At two-fifteen she decided there wasn't any reason to hang around at home anymore and so she left. By the time she arrived at the hospital, she was positively wilting.

He forgot. He didn't forget; he changed his mind. But no, Cassie said he wouldn't do that. What could have happened?

Victor had the day off on Sunday, and at least that was a relief. Since she'd arrived early, she handed in her resignation, stopped at the pharmacy, then went down to put her purse in her locker and got to work.

After a long, intense afternoon, she finally managed to get a coffee break and went to relax for a few precious moments in the doctor's lounge.

And stopped in the doorway. There on the rectangular table in the middle of the room were three long, shiny boxes tied with wide pink ribbons. She walked over slowly, saw the envelope on top with her name on it, and tore it open.

The card inside read: "Got tied up on the phone. Something I couldn't get out of. Am frustrated as hell, and I miss you. All my love, Chance."

Inside the boxes were three dozen long-stemmed red roses, their petals lush, perfect, heavy with fragrance. She held them to her nose and breathed in their scent for a long time. Then she tucked her note carefully away, asked one of the nurses on duty to get her something to put the flowers in, and waltzed back to work.

CHAPTER EIGHT

"Do I LOOK all right?" Mary asked, nose-to-nose with her reflection in her bathroom mirror as she checked her makeup for any minuscule signs of unevenness. There were none, for what she wore was subtle and painstakingly applied. A light application of peach blusher along her high, delicate cheekbones, the merest touch of dark blue eye shadow making her eyes gleam like aquamarines, one coating of mascara and lip gloss.

"You look great." Tim lounged against the open doorway, lanky arms folded across his chest as he studied her. "Big date, huh?"

Mary fluffed tawny bangs anxiously and inspected her small, even white teeth, then sighed. She wasn't going to make her appearance any better by fretting. This was as good as it got. "You could say that."

It was early Tuesday evening. Chance was picking her up in a few minutes to take her to dinner with his parents at their restaurant. Caught in the whirlwind of working out her notice at the hospital, she hadn't had time to see him since their explosive date on Saturday night, although she had talked with him on the phone Monday and earlier that day. Both conversations had been long and warm, and had left her filled with longing. Both times he had told her he loved her. She needed to look into his eyes and see that it was true.

"You've really fallen for him, haven't you?" Tim said.

Mary smoothed the skirt of her ankle-length, red shirtwaist dress, checked her matching low-heeled pumps, then glanced at Tim as she turned away from the mirror. What should she say to him? Chance had not brought up marriage since Saturday; true to his word, he was giving her time to think. They had nothing agreed upon between them, and Tim liked him so much that if anything went wrong and they didn't get together, she knew he would be much more disappointed than he had been about Victor.

She didn't want to raise his hopes, but she didn't want to lie, either. She said simply, "Yes."

His eyes lit up and he grinned happily. "That's so cool," he said. "And he likes you an awful lot. He asked all sorts of questions about you when we went to the fair. You two could really be something."

There was no way to keep his hopes from being raised. He was busy doing that all on his own. She sighed, "Oh, Timmy. I—I guess we'll just have to wait and see."

He scooped up her purse from the foot of the bed and handed it to her. "Sure." He paused, then said awkwardly, "Don't mind what happened on Saturday. I think Grampa does like him, too. He's just being careful, you know?"

"We all need to be careful, Timmy."

Fifteen minutes later she opened the front door to greet Chance, and that wise admonition flew right out of her head.

The sight of him hit her like a blow to her middle. Dressed in a tailored navy blue suit, cream shirt and dark tie, his blond hair smooth and gleaming, he

radiated masculinity and elegance. The suit was unex-
pectedly sober, conservative, the classic lines high-
lighting the corded grace in the bones of his wrists,
hands and the chiseled planes of his face. It was such
a definitive change from the tough, teasing man she
had come to know, she felt her perspective on him
shift again. He was a man with so many facets, a man
who had struggled to come to terms with himself and
had won, it would take a lifetime to get to know him
properly.

He looked at her, compulsively down the entire
length of her body, and his hazel gaze lit with a fierce,
smoky flame. The bones of his face seemed to com-
press and sharpen, and suddenly the conservative elegance of the suit became just what it was: a
camouflage for other people in a civilized setting.
Somehow without even speaking he managed to strip
himself of the veneer and reveal to her what lay hidden
underneath. For her sake it was leashed for the
moment, that predator that had slept for so long and
had only now stirred slumberously back to life, and
it was ravenous.

Mary clung to the doorknob as his dark voice,
melted chocolate and gravel, curled into her. "Mary,
you are beautiful. Do I need to come in and make
polite noises to your family?"

She shook her head dumbly; she had no words.

He held out his hand to her. "Then we should go."

Only then did she truly understand. He was mag-
nificent and he was terrifying. He would take her
outside of the self she had known and make her into
something new. She could refuse. She could back into
her house, shut the door on him, and hide in the shell
of her tidy, comfortable life.

Then she smiled, an odd, helpless smile. The only way she could refuse was if she could somehow journey out of the vast labyrinth that was him, for she knew she was inside him.

Her soul had not gone on a shelf. He had wrapped himself around her protectively, courageously, and had put her in the safest, most precious place he knew of: behind his barriers against the world, deep into the very heart of him. She knew it as surely as she could see the remnants of Saturday's vulnerable questioning in his eyes. The predator was awake and ravenous for her. Her had himself sternly, adamantly on a leash for her. Everything he had said and done in the past week had been for her.

Mary could no more refuse him than she could refuse to breathe. She reached out her hand and was encompassed, and gently he drew her out of her house, and she came to him dancing.

The Falcon Club was one of the premier restaurants in Cherry Bay. Somehow it managed to combine artistry with unpretentiousness. The cuisine on offer had an international flair, and the decor was very plain, with pieces from local painters hanging on the walls, glossy hardwood floors and white-covered tables adorned with candles and fresh flowers. It was one of Mary's favorite places to dine, but she had never met the owners. She entered the restaurant with her hand tucked snugly into the crook of Chance's arm, viewing everything with a fresh perspective.

He led her over to a table tucked away from the others, in the corner of the restaurant with a breathtaking view of the bay. There was an older couple already seated at the table, drinking wine and talking quietly. They rose to their feet as Chance and Mary approached.

Chance covered her fingers with his, squeezing lightly. "Mary, this is my mom, Carmen, and my dad, Johnny. Mom, Dad—this is Mary Newman. Don't scare her away, will you?"

"For heaven's sake, Chance," said his mother chidingly. "As if we would. If she's not scared away by you, she deserves all our sympathy and support."

Chance grinned and Mary chuckled, looking up into Carmen's face. Chance's mother was a tall, strong-boned woman, with red hair touched gracefully at the temples with silver, Cassie's facial features and Chance's hazel eyes. Those hauntingly familiar eyes were warmly welcoming as they looked at Mary. Suddenly her nervousness fell away, and she glowed with pleasure as she shook the older woman's hand.

Chance's stepfather, Johnny, was a slim, distinguished man, also graying, with an elegantly erect carriage, aquiline features and gentle green eyes. He smoothly interposed himself between Mary and Chance, held out a chair for her, and proceeded to see to her every comfort.

Chance changed course and headed for the chair on the other side of Mary, but his mother beat him to it. He stopped, cocked his head and said, "I think I'm being outmaneuvered."

"Of course you are," said Johnny comfortably, settling back and smiling at the younger man. "We want to talk to you and get to know Mary, not watch you two sink into a world of your own."

Chance frowned mock-seriously, then acquiesced and took the chair opposite Mary. But he glanced at her as he did so, and the ravenous, leashed part of him spoke to her. Later, it said.

Though she was warm, she shivered. Her face shone with wonder and delicious apprehension, and no small bewilderment at what he did to her. Later, she promised.

With that, the predator was content and drew back to wait, and Chance turned to his parents to pretend that he was interested in more commonplace things.

Mary was amazed. Neither Carmen nor Johnny seemed to noticed the pretender in their midst, and they had known him all his life. They laughed heartily at his dry witticisms, and drew Mary out of herself with gracious kindness and a genuine liking. They asked for her opinions and listened with respect to her replies.

As she grew to know them, she could see how they had both had a hand in shaping his character as he'd grown from being a troubled teenager into becoming the man that he was. Chance's own brilliance, hard and cutting as a diamond, could have once been what would have broken him. But the gifts they had given him—his mother's gritty determination, his stepfather's ethics and gentle strength—had saved him from himself.

Even as the excellent meal progressed and she expanded to sparkle under the wise nurturing they showered upon her, one part of her was always intimately aware of the man opposite her. He stalked her with patient silence. He lounged back in a languid manner, and one of his long legs brushed against hers. He talked to his mother about taking Tim to the fair, while his gaze caressed her. He and his stepfather ordered brandy and coffee for dessert, while he reached across the table and carefully refilled her wineglass.

The part of her that was his prey knew it was being hunted. It crouched still and small, considered the possible wisdom of bolting, and knew it would not.

Then somehow the evening was over with, and Carmen and Johnny were saying good-night. Mary shook both their hands and was immensely pleased when the older woman bent to brush her lips against her cheek. "We so enjoyed meeting you, Mary," Carmen said. "You must come to dinner again soon. We'll have a more cozy time of it at our house, and we'd love to meet your family, as well."

"We'll ask Cassie to come, too," Johnny added.

Mary smiled, and the other three paused to drink in her delight. "Oh, I'd like that."

"Next week?" Carmen asked, and she nodded.

Chance strolled around the table to put a hand at the small of her back. The heavy warmth of it seared through the thin material of her dress and seemed to brand her. "We'll arrange for a night when everybody's free," he said. "I'll call you, Mom."

Carmen looked at her son for a long moment, her gaze sober and loving, and that was when Mary discovered that both his parents knew quite well what had really gone on that evening. They knew, accepted, and she realized just how comprehensive their welcome to her had been.

"Thank you for everything," she said quietly.

"I couldn't be more pleased," Carmen answered just as quietly.

She and Chance walked outside, and they both paused on the doorstep of the restaurant for a moment, taking in the fresh night air. The breeze teased at her skirt and licked against her legs. She looked up and said softly, "I liked your parents."

His preoccupied expression vanished, and he focused on her. "They both loved you, but then I knew they would." He paused, staring intently at her, then whispered, "Come back to my place."

Again, it flashed through her: Bolt. Hide. She shoved the thought aside and reached out both arms to him. "Oh, yes, please."

He made a hoarse sound and crushed her to him briefly, a hard, bruising hold. Then he swept an arm around her waist and walked her swiftly to his car.

She was heated, exhilarated. Chance's face, in the dim glow of the dashboard, was like an ageless marble sculpture, the tiny signs of humanity, both temper and humor, smoothed away by the semidarkness. She averted her eyes and watched the road scroll past them.

When they got out of town, he took a side road that wound through the hills bordering the shore of the lake. On either side of the road, houses nestled in land covered by forest. After a few minutes, he signaled and turned left into the driveway of a two-story, wood-shingled house. Mary could see, through the break in the trees, dark, glimmering water.

The engine died into silence. For a moment neither one of them moved. She clasped her hands tightly together in her lap, refused to look at him, and tried hard to breathe normally.

This was excruciating. Saturday night, in spite of Victor, had been filled with so much magical promise, and now she wondered if she might have made some terrible mistake. She opened her mouth to ask him to take her home, but just then he shifted and put a hand over hers.

"I bought you a present yesterday," he said quietly. Huge, terrified blue eyes turned to look at him, and he almost groaned.

Some of the awful tension that had gripped her eased somewhat as curiosity pricked. "What is it?"

"Come on inside—I have a deck that overlooks the beach. We can have coffee out there if you like."

He sounded so calm and unruffled. Relief and disappointment warred inside her. How could he act as if this was just another date—maybe he really meant for her to meet his parents, visit awhile, and then to take her home. Maybe her imagination had been overactive. Maybe that was a good thing. She trailed behind him to the house, tangled up in herself.

The interior of the house was paneled with the same natural wood as the outside, and furnished with plain leather furniture, plenty of shelves filled with books, and large framed photographs of varying landscapes on the walls. The overall impression was undeniably masculine, but comfortable, homey.

Mary had stopped dead ten feet in from the front door. Chance appeared not to notice as he strolled easily toward the back of the house, shedding suit jacket and tie as he went. He flashed her a brief smile over his shoulder. "Feel free to look around while I make the coffee."

"Thank you," she said, bewildered. He disappeared around a corner.

In the space left by his absence, she had time to think, and she discovered she was curious. Wandering through the house was like a private treasure hunt, as she gleaned clues about him wherever she looked.

One of the downstairs rooms had been converted into an office. She peeked inside briefly, saw a desktop computer, laser printer, filing cabinets, shelves with textbooks and journals, a dart board obviously well used. That made her smile to herself. The room was the most cluttered in the house, scattered with stacks of papers and maps. The desk chair was also leather and somewhat battered, bearing the impression of his body.

He liked classics, biographies and mysteries, puzzles and strategy games. A handwoven afghan was thrown carelessly over the back of the couch. A polished wood chessboard with pieces carved from dark and light onyx sat on an end table near the fireplace in the living room. The bathroom was neat and somewhat spare, but she smiled to see the aqua-colored shower curtain that bore the pattern of stylized mermaids and seashells. She opened the medicine cabinet, spotted a bottle of after-shave, and inhaled the familiar spicy scent.

She gave the shadowed staircase leading to the second floor one curious glance, but at the thought of exploring up there, her courage failed. She scuttled into the hall toward the kitchen and bumped into him as he rounded the corner.

His hands curled around her elbows to steady her as he chuckled. "Do you like the place?"

His hair had fallen over his brow. She spread her hands over his chest and smiled up at him. "Yes, it's lovely. Do—do you own or rent? Oh—the coffee smells . . . nice." His eyes had started to crinkle. Shut up! She closed her mouth with a snap and fell silent.

His fingers slid along her bare skin. "I haven't been here long, just a few months, and I could be persuaded to move—for the right reasons. And the coffee's just done. Would you like some?''

She nodded, and he took her into the kitchen, walled on one side with bricks. A white countertop separated the kitchen from the dining room. He had opened the glass doors leading onto the deck, where lights around the rail illuminated redwood tables and chairs. The murmuring sound of the lake drifted in.

Chance poured two cups of coffee and added cream to hers. Mary paused, her attention diverted by the high stack of dishes in the drainer. She started to smile, guessing that he had cleaned the house thoroughly that day. Then she noticed the dining-room table, which seated eight, and the deck furniture, with room for at least eight, as well. That was a great deal of seating space for a single man, unless he entertained often.

She wondered who his acquaintances here were, and whether he had had people over the night before. He hadn't mentioned anything to her over the phone. Her gaze fell on the sideboard in the dining room, which was stacked with papers and files and empty ashtrays. For the first time she noticed a faint odor of stale cigar and cigarette smoke in that part of the house.

Chance followed her gaze, drew a breath, and put a hand on her arm. ''Want to go out on the deck?''

Her attention came back to him with a start. ''All right.'' He carried their full cups out carefully, and she followed, feeling an odd tenderness at how he bent his head so studiously to the small task. ''Chance?'' He set the cups down on one of the tables and turned to her. ''I quit my job. I—wanted to tell you in person. I gave them two weeks' notice on Sunday.''

His calm stripped away. "You did?" She nodded, and he took a swift, uncontrolled step toward her, then stopped and said hoarsely, "Mary, for God's sake—are you going to marry me or not?"

She made a noise—it was supposed to be a laugh— and nodded again.

He finished the small journey to her, took hold of her shoulders, and hauled her against him. "I've been half out of my mind," he growled.

Her head fell back. At the same time she said, "I told you I would on Saturday—I didn't need time—"

His eyes were ferocious with joy. "Yes, you did need time."

She just shook her head and whispered, "You'll have to start trusting me to know what I want."

He paused tensely, then whispered back, "I trust you, and you'd better be prepared to trust me. Even the parts of me you don't know about yet."

"I love you," she moaned.

His fingers dug into her shoulders, compressing bones together, then he sank his hands into her loose hair greedily, lifting the heavy mass to bury his face in it. "I love you. I will always love you. That's it, you're mine—you said so. Swear it, Mary."

"I swear." She clung to his lean waist, face buried in his chest.

Silence, filled with the quiet sound of the water and the scattered song of crickets. He said very quietly, "You're everything, Mary."

"You're mine, too."

She felt the murmured words shudder through him. "Yes. I swear it. Oh—" He lifted his head. "Damn— your present. I put it in the chair I was going to make you sit in." She blinked up at him, and he flashed her a crooked grin. "I hope you like it."

She looked at the chairs, saw the wrapped box in one of them, and wobbled over giddily to snatch it up. It was so small it looked like... She tore the silvery paper off and yanked open the top. Inside, nestled against dark velvet, was a large diamond ring surrounded by sapphires. It was so obviously and undeniably an engagement ring. There was no mistaking what that ring was. She held it against her chest and bowed her head over it.

Unsteady laughter threaded his voice. "Here, let me put it on you."

She stuck her hand out and covered her trembling mouth as she watched him slip the ring on her finger. He'd guessed the size well so that it fitted snugly enough, but still she closed her hand into a fist. He cupped her fist, staring down at it, and said, "Soon."

After all the whirling her head had done over the past week, at last she could see the future with perfect clarity. "After I finish working out my notice? That soon?"

A muscle bunched in his jaw. "Yes. Do you mind not having a large wedding?"

She reached up to stroke the hair back from his brow. "I think a wedding with just our families would be wonderful. Maybe we could have it in my grandfather's horrible garden."

His eyes gleamed with mischief. "With the rotting boathouse and the pavilions."

"That silly bridge."

"The aroma of the swamp."

She giggled. "The swamp doesn't stink. Much. And anyway, we have acres and acres—we could find some way to stay upwind of it."

He laughed out loud and clasped her to him. He was such a different man from the one she had first met. Cleared of cynicism, stripped of barriers, he was boyish and severe, mature and youthful, and his face was a miracle. "Your grandfather's going to pack a shotgun to make sure I take my vows seriously," he remarked dryly.

She nestled into him. "And your parents will send me a sympathy card."

He passed a hand over her hair. "Cassie'll cry. She always cries at weddings. Lord, she'll be mad at me for that."

"Timmy's easy," she said dreamily. "He'll be over the moon."

He turned serious, taut. He slid a hand between their bodies, pressed it flat against her belly, and murmured throatily in her ear, "We could try to make it a real shotgun wedding."

For a moment she didn't get his meaning. Then it sank in. Shotgun weddings were for pregnant brides. Realization bolted through her, shaking the strength out of her knees and shortening her breath. Pregnant, with a part of him inside her. The idea, first planted by him on Saturday, had taken root and grown.

"Oh, God." She tilted her hot face up, and he rubbed his cheek against hers slowly, eyes closed.

"I want a baby girl, with your hair and eyes and a startled, innocent little face," he whispered fiercely. "I want a boy like Tim. I want twins, dammit. I'm so hungry for what we're going to have together. I'm impatient for it, Mary, but if you're not ready I can wait if I have to."

She covered his mouth. "No. We're not going to have it, Chance. We have it now. I want it, too."

His breath hissed, and his head reared back. He stared into her eyes, saw confirmation there, and plummeted down to devour her mouth.

He would have knocked her off her feet had he not been holding her so tightly. She wrapped her arms around his neck and kissed him back wildly. He sucked hard on her lower lip, muttering incoherently, and she pulsed in reply, a startling, violent, involuntary reaction.

He molded himself around her, hardened and roused, bowing her back over one arm while he learned the delicate curves and hollows of her body. Needing to feel his skin against hers, she fumbled at the buttons on his shirt. She was shaking so much that they seemed like an incredibly insurmountable task—until one fell open, and she could see the shadow of his rapid heartbeat in the base of his neck. He was sheened in sweat.

She bent forward, put her open mouth to that luscious golden skin and licked him.

A groan wrenched out of him, and he put a hand at the back of her head and pressed her mouth harder against him. Mindlessly she explored that furred, hard-muscled expanse with lips and tongue. His powerful body shook.

Then he grasped hold of her and pulled away. He was gasping; she stared at him bemusedly. Did he mean to let go of her? She didn't think she could stand on her own.

"Not here, baby. Come on." He picked her up and carried her inside, pausing only to shut and lock the balcony door. She didn't know or care where he was going. She lay back in his arms and stared up at him. The planes and hollows of his face were bladelike, and his brilliant eyes glittered. He was the most beautiful thing she had ever seen, but his sheer rampant male aggression was frightening.

Then he looked at her, and his expression underwent a dramatic change as he laid her tenderly down on his bed. The room was shadowy, lit only by moonlight and the distant glow from downstairs.

Her tawny hair lay in a fan around her, and the red dress fell in a tangle around her legs. Her eyes were immense, her face shaken.

He paused to stare down at her. She was so fragile and precious he could barely breathe. Nothing in his life had prepared him adequately for this moment, for the exquisite mixture of fear and love and faith in her eyes. He needed to shield her from everything painful in the world, protect her, surround her with her dreams. His dreams. Theirs. He crooned and pressed his lips gently to her neck. "Mary. Precious. Trust me."

Her fingers pressed lightly against his cheekbone. She whispered, "I do."

He straddled her while still nuzzling softly at her neck, bracing himself on his elbows on either side of her head. Her eyelids drooped. He was over and around her, covering her with himself. She was in that warm, safe cave again, and she never wanted to come out.

With one hand he gently teased the buttons of her dress aside. "I love you," he said in her ear. "I need you.'' Then the last part of her dress fell away, revealing her slender torso covered with a red lace teddy, and he trembled. ''Oh, Mary—oh, baby, you are so lovely.''

She arched up to him hungrily, gripping his forearms. ''I love you,'' she whimpered.

Carefully he uncovered her, so carefully he undressed himself and pressed his tight, hot weight down upon her. He kissed and kissed her all over, nibbling at her breasts, stroking between her legs, while the moon lit the curve of his shoulder and line of his back in silver. It shone on the side of his face as he bowed over her, sparkling on wetness.

Tears? Was he crying?

What could she give him? She gave him herself. ''There's never been anyone but you. There's only you.''

He sucked air and came inside her, and the piercing shock of being filled by him made her claw at the sheets and cry out.

He held still, pressing her into the bed, and with hands and broken voice he soothed her, until the pain passed and she could hold him again.

His head bowed onto the pillow beside her. He was so rigid, she was afraid he would break into pieces. Carefully she stretched, straining to meet him, and when that didn't break his rigidity, she whispered, ''Please.''

He sobbed then, clutching her, and started to move, and it was so liquid, so exquisitely right, that the hot curl of passion wound tighter in her with every slow pumping stroke of his hips. She twisted underneath him, whining, and he fisted a hand into her tangled hair, pinning her down. She raked her fingernails down his back frenziedly and sank her teeth into his shoulder.

His control shattered. He slammed into her, head thrown back, the tendons of his neck etched. She stared into his contorted face, then shook explosively into climax.

"You—are—mine," he gritted.

She touched his ferocious face and gasped, "Yes."

At that he thrust into her one last time, and broke into a convulsive shuddering. Shakenly she murmured to him, wrapping both arms and legs around him tight, bringing him back to himself again, bringing him home.

CHAPTER NINE

OVERCOME by exhaustion, cradled close against Chance's chest, she fell asleep and dreamed of being surrounded. Every time she moved, the warm cocoon followed, curving around her slender frame with intimate sensitivity. Someone murmured love words to her in a dark, low voice, and brushed aside her heavy mass of hair to nuzzle the nape of her neck. Caught in the silken threads of the dream cocoon, she did not fully awaken but stretched with languid, incoherent pleasure as she was stroked delicately all over her body.

When at last she opened her eyes, the pale silver light of early morning illuminated a window. She blinked at the sight, not recognizing the window or the trees outside. She was curled on her side and pinned by a warm weight.

Chance. She followed the long, tanned arm that curved around her torso to its source. His face was relaxed in sleep, the edges smoothed. He was lying on her hair. As she watched, he nestled into the long, soft strands and drew her closer against his wide, furred chest.

Warmth flooded her. Sore muscles murmured of last night's pleasure. His heavy thigh was pressed between hers. She was pinned and couldn't go anywhere even if she'd wanted to, which she didn't. Why consider going anywhere else? Where was there to go?

She had arrived. She had come home finally, and it had been worth the long years of waiting.

Could they have made a baby last night? She knew the chances were fairly slim after just one night, but oh, she hoped so. She wanted a daughter with his dancing hazel eyes. She wanted a son with his wicked grin.

She craned her neck and nibbled at his lips. His hand came up to cup her face, eyes slitting half-open as he kissed her back.

"Good morning," she murmured.

He pulled her hips back against his and kissed down the side of her neck. "Good morning, precious. Did we say we were getting married this morning?"

Her heavy head fell back to the pillow as sexuality stirred. "Mmm. N-no, I think we said in two weeks." Her breath caught. He had slid one hand between her thighs and was probing her gently with those long, callused fingers. "Oh! That's—that's nice."

He growled softly deep in his chest, a lion's purr, and muttered, "So we opted for the long engagement. Want to change your mind?"

She stretched deliciously, feeling him harden against her hip. "But everybody would be disappointed."

"So? We could get a special license, or fly to Las Vegas." His hand roamed, reaching up to trace circles around her nipple as he crooned in her ear, "Wouldn't you like to get married by Elvis? I've heard several of them are alive down there."

She laughed weakly. "But what about Timmy? I couldn't look my grandfather in the face afterward— and Cassie, and your parents?"

"We'll buy plane tickets for all of them. Tim'd like Vegas." He rolled her onto her back, captured the nipple he'd been teasing with his mouth and began to suckle. Her eyes fluttered shut and she gripped his head while the deep, sensual hunger began to build. After a time he leaned his forehead against her, breathing hard. "All right. Maybe not Vegas. But I won't be without you for two weeks, dammit. So are you going to move in here, or should I come there?"

She nuzzled at his hair, running her fingers through it. It was so much more silken than hers. In the morning light the top strands were the palest of golds. "Why don't we ask my grandfather?"

"He'll have to either put up with me, or face losing you," he said quietly. "That'll be a hard choice for him."

"I love him, but I won't be without you, either," she answered just as quietly. She framed his lean face, looking deeply into his eyes. His morning growth of beard was as golden as the rest of him, tickling her fingers, and his eyes were bottomless, ringed with rich flecks of brown, blue and green. She felt as if she were falling into him. "He'll have to come to terms with it, Chance. Sooner or later he would face losing me anyway."

"I love you," he said from the back of his throat. "I love you."

The words pierced her with the same power as the first time she'd ever heard him utter them. She wrapped both arms around his neck, cradling his head against her breast. "I love you," she whispered.

"Let's go to the county-city building later and order a marriage license."

"All right."

"When do you have to be at work?" He teased a wavy lock of her tawny hair over her shoulder and rubbed it against his cheek.

"Three o'clock." She rediscovered the width of his shoulders, the beautiful interplay of the muscles in his back.

"We have time, then. We can call my parents and Cassie. They won't be surprised. Cassie helped me pick out your ring. When I take you back home, we can talk to Tim and your grandfather."

"That's a good idea—oh, God!" She let her head fall back on the pillow.

He propped himself on his elbows and stared down at her. "What?"

"I have to call them. I didn't come home last night, and they'll be so worried."

"Ssh, now," he said soothingly. "They must not be awake yet, or they would have found my number in the book and called." He glanced at his bedside clock. "It's still very early. You can leave it for a couple of hours—until eight-thirty or so. If they're awake by then, they'll probably just think you're still in bed."

Chance was right, she realized. That was exactly what they would think. After all, she'd never spent the night with a man before. She relaxed, her gaze caught by the kite pattern of hair on his chest. She followed the arrow of it down his flat abdomen until it disappeared in the tangle of blankets around his hips.

He noticed the direction of her gaze, and his eyes darkened. Bending down to press quick, light kisses against her mouth, he whispered, "Mary."

"Hmm." Her lips caressed his.

"Mary, are you very sore?" He licked at her collarbone. One of his hands had started to roam over her again, hungrily.

She arched up to him. "Not—not very."

"We could wait if you like," he purred. He touched her between her thighs again, and she convulsed.

"No!" She dug her nails into him. "No, you don't, you devil."

He started to laugh, and she pushed him back against the pillows, exploring him as he had explored her, with lips and tongue and shaking hands.

Soon his laughter stopped, and he guided her to what brought him pleasure, tutoring her with hoarse, whispered encouragement. She was unskilled but eager to learn and thrilled to find him writhing under her light, tentative touch.

His head turned restlessly, the bones of his face stark. She paused, looking up at his blazing eyes in wonder. He grasped hold of her by the hips, lifted her over him, and as she automatically parted her legs to straddle him, he thrust up inside her.

She arched and cried out.

He withdrew, fingers digging into the soft flesh of her thighs, then arched again to fill her. She clung to his rigid forearms, shaking violently.

He paused, forcing her to stillness while he devoured every aspect of her: the long, tangled hair that clung in strands to her dampened neck, the wild, predatory hunger in her face, the undulating grace of her torso, the jutting delicacy of her slight, rounded breasts.

She clawed at his arms, grinding down on him as she sobbed, "Don't stop."

He slammed into her again and again, gasping her name, and she bowed over him, twisting as she climaxed. Her inner muscles tightened on him, and he splintered helplessly.

He clutched her shivering shoulders as she fell down on him. She burrowed mindlessly, seeking the warm, safe cave, and he wrapped himself around her, stroking the back of her head tenderly, until her shivering had stopped and all was peaceful again.

An hour later Mary stepped out of the shower, toweled herself dry, and slipped on Chance's blue terry-cloth robe. It would be thigh-length on him; on her the hem came to past her knees.

She loved their size difference. She loved everything about him. She loved everything in the world. She was drunk and she knew it, and if she was very, very fortunate she might live the rest of her life without ever sobering up. She straightened the shower curtain, giggled at the mermaid print on it, and waltzed out of the bathroom.

The robe smelled like him too. She hugged herself delightedly, thinking, I'll surprise him by cooking his breakfast while he showers. A mushroom and cheese omelette maybe, or French toast. I know he has a sweet tooth. He enjoyed his caramel apple at the fair. Or—she looked at the stairway and started to chuckle again as she remembered what Cassie had said about his lack of culinary skills. Maybe I'd just better wait to see what kind of food supplies he has before planning anything too ambitious.

She slipped into the kitchen and started to root through his cupboards. There were several different kinds of soup, packaged noodles, a box of Melba toast, a jar of beluga caviar, a small can of oysters and some black olives. And a bottle of Scotch, and another one of Courvoisier brandy. She put her tongue between her teeth, amused and not very surprised, and went to see what tale the refrigerator had to tell her.

The freezer held eight microwave dinners, containers of gourmet ice cream, a bag of ice and a bottle of vodka. She squatted and rummaged through the rest of the fridge in fascination. There were vast quantities of leftover Chinese take-out boxes, filled with everything from fried rice and moo goo guy pan to sweet and sour shrimp.

There was no bread to be found anywhere, ergo no toast. No eggs, either. She did find a half gallon of milk, a tub of margarine, a can of coffee and several containers of flavored low-fat yogurt. Sighing, she rocked back on her heels and nibbled at a fingernail. She supposed all that yogurt was vaguely encouraging about some kind of nutritional sense.

When Mary didn't come back to the bedroom, Chance slipped on a pair of light cotton shorts and went in search of her. She wasn't in the bathroom, either. He strode through the downstairs, unsettled, and as he rounded the corner to the dining room and kitchen area, he glanced around quickly and noticed that the refrigerator door was open.

"Mary?" he asked.

Up popped a small hand from behind the counter, and short fingers waggled at him. The sleeve of the blue robe flopped around her wrist like a giant bell. It was her left hand. He paused to appreciate how prettily the diamond ring flashed on her finger, and then strolled over to lean his elbows on the counter and regard her.

She smiled up at him. "I was going to surprise you with breakfast."

He smiled back. The robe also made her blue eyes glimmer like jewels, and it was beginning to slip off one fine-boned shoulder. Everything about her was perfection in miniature, even down to the coltish length of her leg and the shapely curve of her ankle. She had painted her toenails red to match the outfit she'd worn last night; her toes curled like tiny pink seashells on the tiled floor.

He decided he liked her wearing his clothes. "What a nice idea," he told her, then chuckled as she shrugged and gestured helplessly at the contents of the fridge. "As you've probably deduced, I'm no chef."

She shut the refrigerator door, straightened, then leaned on the counter toward him. "I love to cook. Since I can't make you breakfast, I'll fix Sunday dinner for you if you like."

His eyes lit up. "Sunday dinner? Do you know how to cook ham?"

She nodded. "How about ham with pineapple slices and a brown sugar glaze? I could do crescent rolls and mashed potatoes."

He couldn't resist. "And do you know how to make peach pie?"

She nearly laughed out loud at the look of helpless longing on his face. "Yes," she promised, and he closed his eyes dreamily. "A peach pie, too." She caressed his cheek. "I'm looking forward to cooking lots for you," she said softly, then tweaked his nose. "If you're good."

His eyes snapped open. She twinkled at him merrily. He stared at her for a moment, enchanted. Looking at her in this playful mood was like recovering a cherished part of himself, long misplaced and nearly forgotten. It was almost painful how much he needed her.

He shook himself. "Hey," he joked, "be careful with that nose. I'm saving it for you to lead me around by it."

Her laughter was light and silvery. "I'm looking forward to that, too."

He curled a hand around the back of her head and pulled her close for a kiss. She returned it enthusiastically. He drew away reluctantly, taking a deep breath. "I'd better go shower."

She smiled up at him. "All right. While you're doing that, I could . . . I don't know, heat up some of the Chinese?" He made a face and she giggled. "By the way, there's an awful lot of it. Did you have a dinner party recently?"

He nodded. "Sort of. I had people over on Monday night."

"I started wondering if there might be anyone you would like to invite to the wedding," she went on, then paused. He hadn't mentioned having company over when they'd talked on the phone.

"I'll think about it," he said absently. "There are some people from the university I'd like you to meet."

"I'm sure I'll like them." She searched his eyes, not sure what she was sensing.

"I have some things I want to talk to you about," he said. He bent forward and kissed her again, hard. "It's nothing to worry about. Look, why don't you just make coffee while I shower? I'll take you to breakfast after we talk, and then we'll go see Tim and Grampa." He smiled.

She nodded. "All right."

He left, and she found filter papers and pulled the coffee out of the fridge, wondering what he might have to talk about that made him turn so serious. There was old coffee in the machine from the night before. Smiling reminiscently, she washed the carafe, looking out of the window over the sink. Their two cups were on the table where they'd left them, still full of dark liquid. She went out the sliding doors to fetch them.

On her way back inside, she noticed the stacks of files on the sideboard again and paused. Well, they were right out there for anyone to see. She cocked her head, listening. She could hear the distant sound of the shower running.

She could just ask him. Chance, what are all those files for? Do they have something to do with the people you had over on Monday? In fact, she would ask him the minute he returned. In the meantime, she put the cups on the dining-room table, sidled over, and reached out a forefinger to flip open one of the files.

The phone rang in the kitchen, and she jumped guiltily and put her hand behind her back. Then she looked around for a clock. Oh, God, what time is it? Could that be Grampa or Tim? She hurried to snatch up the receiver. "Hello?"

There was a slight pause, the line crackling with interference. "Mr. Armstrong, please," said a man's voice through the interference.

The formal title jarred her a little. It was a stranger. Not Tim, not Grampa. Relieved, she said, "He's busy. May I ask who's calling?"

Another slight pause. "This is Andrew Duncan, ma'am. Who'm I speaking to?"

"Mary Newman." It must be a long-distance call, maybe from overseas. She smiled a little. Maybe he was one of those work contacts of Chance's. She confessed with shy pride, "I'm his fiancée."

"Is that so?" His voice warmed. "Well, congratulations. Could you have him call me just as soon as he can?"

"Certainly—oh, wait a minute." She turned as Chance, dressed in cutoffs and a white T-shirt, entered the room. He was freshly shaved, and his combed hair was damp. "Here he is now."

"Thank you."

She handed the receiver to Chance, who gave her a questioning look. "Andrew Duncan," she mouthed, and went to retrieve the coffee cups from the table while he spoke quietly into the phone.

He moved into the dining room to talk while Mary washed the cups and saucers, thinking ahead to when he got off the phone. She wouldn't wait any longer but had to call home right away, even if she woke someone up. She hated the thought of their finding out she wasn't home and then panicking.

She looked over her shoulder. He had finished his conversation and was leaning against the counter, watching her intently. She smiled. "Lord, all I've got to wear is my red dress. Chance, I'm worried about Grampa and Tim worrying. We'd better go home first and talk to them. I can cook us something to eat there. Is that all right?"

"Hmm?"

His gaze really focused on her, and she realized he'd not been listening.

The smile drained from her face. "Is something wrong?"

He ran his fingers through his hair. "I'm sorry, baby. Nothing's really wrong. I was thinking. We're going to have to postpone our plans for today, sweetheart."

"But why?"

"There's an emergency conference in Washington that I need to cover."

She blinked. "What do you mean, you need to cover?" She sounded very stupid as she grappled for the meaning of what he'd said. "Just like that? I thought you'd taken the summer off."

"This is different." He rubbed the back of his neck and shifted restlessly. "I've got an inside contact at the White House who won't talk to anybody but me."

"Is that who Andrew is?"

He smiled belatedly and shook his head. "I'm sorry, I can't say."

She shook her head in bemusement, too, forehead wrinkled. "All right. When will you be back?"

"It's hard to say." He turned to watch her closely. "I might only be a day or two."

Only? She smiled again, past her disappointment. "Do you have to leave right away? Couldn't we talk to Tim and my grandfather first, and then you could go?"

"I'd better leave as soon as I can get a flight."

"I could go ahead and talk to them on my own."

"Why don't you wait until we can do that together?"

"Yes, I'd rather do that. How soon will you know how long you're going to be?"

He hesitated. "I'll definitely call you tonight, precious, but I just don't know enough right now."

She drooped; she couldn't help it. "That sounds sensible."

He smiled and came to cup her elbows. "I know, I hate it, too. I'll try to come home tomorrow night, since you're not working."

She slid her hands up his forearms. Then what he said sank in. "You'll try? You mean you may not be able to? What kind of an 'emergency conference' is this?"

He sighed. "There's not much I can tell you."

She frowned and fiddled with the edges of his T-shirt sleeves, pleating them between her fingers. Stop asking, she told herself. Privileged information, Mary. You know that. You do that when patients tell you secrets.

Only, your patients aren't "inside" contacts in the White House, and you don't have to listen to them for days on end, talking about potentially dangerous situations. War. She sucked in a breath, glancing past him to the stack of files. "Is it serious?"

He paused for a moment, then said slowly, "I'm walking a line, Mary, between telling you things and breaking confidences. There's been trouble again in the Balkans, and some professors at the university have family over there. I checked with my contact in Washington to find out what was going on and he called back this morning with confirmation." He stared hard into her eyes. "I really hate to go, but I need to dig into this personally. You're going to have to trust me when I tell you not to worry."

She studied his face thoughtfully for a moment. He said he hated to go, but he didn't act like it. He already seemed to be half-gone, thinking ahead. There was an eagerness about his mannerisms. Something ephemeral was slipping from her grasp.

"Can you tell me this?" she asked. She would decide when she would start worrying. "Are the professors' families in danger?"

"No, no, it's not that bad yet." He squeezed her arms. "I need to go pack. Pour me some coffee?"

"Of course. I'll bring it up."

He bent to kiss her forehead. "Thanks, sugar."

Mary turned to frown at the coffeemaker as he left. She got clean cups from the cupboard, trying to shake the feeling of letdown and anxiety.

How innocuous it all sounded. Just going to cover a conference in Washington, honey. Don't worry about it. If it wasn't something really serious, why was he going? And what happened to "I can't do without you"?

She bit her lip. He was going because it was serious, and his sense of responsibility wouldn't allow him to stay away. And if it was serious, it could get worse, and what if he decided he had to "dig into things" right at the source?

For the first time she realized fully that she had agreed to marry a man who hadn't decided to settle down. Because no matter how much he whitewashed all the implications of his position, he was not just a teacher. She thought he had made the decision to settle down; she believed that even he'd thought that. But all it took was one phone call, and he was upstairs packing, eager to leave.

Other situations like this would come up. He would get midnight calls that he couldn't tell her about. Visitors would come to discuss things with him that she couldn't hear; they would be polite and respectful, but with secrets in their eyes.

And worst of all, she would never know when he might leave again without notice, or how long he would be gone.

All of a sudden she was very cold. She gripped the edges of the robe and pulled it tight under her chin.

The phone rang again, startling her badly. She answered it and said unsteadily, "Hello?"

Her grandfather's voice, gruff and cheerful. "So you're not dead."

She held the receiver away and stared at it in perplexity for a few seconds. Then, cautiously, she put it back to her ear and said, "No. I was going to call. I just didn't know if you'd be up yet. I'm sorry, were you worried?"

"I was planning to get worried if nobody answered." His voice gentled. "Are you okay, kiddo?"

Tears pricked in her eyes. "I don't know," she quavered.

A pause. "I'll kill him. I'm on my way."

She clung to the receiver. "No, no! It's not—whatever you're thinking. We got engaged, Grampa, and oh, it's too much to talk about over the phone. I'll be coming home soon. Can we talk when I get there?"

"Of course we can. You'll be all right until then?"

"Yes. I love you."

"Love you, too. See you soon."

She heard him muttering as he hung up. Then, like an automaton, she poured a cup of coffee, leaving it black the way Chance liked it, and concentrated on carrying it carefully up the stairs.

In the doorway she paused, staring.

Chance was wearing a black formal suit and white shirt. Gold cuff links winked at his wrists, and the severity of the suit emphasized the lines of his powerful body. He was tucking a toiletry kit into a leather duffel bag. As she watched, he pivoted and strode to the closet to pull out a few more items of clothing. The light from the window glinted off the burnished gold of his hair. His chiseled face was hardened, and his intelligent hazel eyes were piercing.

Hot coffee splashed onto her hand. As always, he was beautiful, but he bore no resemblance to the gentle, passionate lover from earlier that morning. This man had a razor edge that cut, and she didn't know him.

Carefully she carried the cup to the bedside table; carefully she set it down and nursed her burned hand.

"Thanks, sugar," he said from behind her, and he moved her hair aside to kiss the back of her neck.

She shivered at the light caress and her head ducked lower. She didn't dare turn to look at him. She said quietly, "Chance, what if I'm pregnant?"

He closed his arms around her in a snug embrace, resting his chin on top of her head. His voice was quiet, too, and cautious. "I thought you wanted to be. Are you having second thoughts?"

She pressed her hand to her trembling lips and said painfully, "Yes. What if I'm pregnant and you decide you need to go to the Balkans?"

A long pause. He said patiently, "I'm not going to the Balkans, Mary. I'm going to a nice hotel in Washington, and I'll call you as often as I can. Please stop worrying."

"Don't talk about specifics, Chance. We said we wanted children—not just one. And even one pregnancy takes nine months. What if I'm pregnant, and you need to go somewhere? What then?"

He rocked her gently. "Then we'll have to deal with each situation as it comes up."

She closed her eyes and leaned back against him. "I—I don't think I can live with dealing with each situation as it comes up."

He sighed sharply, released her and started to pace. She turned to watch him. Even though his inherent prowling grace was something she'd grown used to, she remembered how it had unsettled her when they'd first met.

"You don't think you can live with it," he repeated flatly.

She straightened her shoulders. "No. We've never talked about this before, and we have to. If something explodes in Asia or Africa or South America, are you really going to be content to stay here? Would you expect me to come along sometimes? Would you expect me to wait at home? Do you have any idea?"

He jammed a pair of pants into his bag, then swung around to face her, his expression grim. "You knew what I was from the first day we met. Why are you acting as if all of this just occurred to you?"

"Because I've just invested myself in you." She clasped her hands together. "And I'm scared."

"You weren't scared of this last night." A cold edge had entered his voice. "You said you would trust me. You said I should trust you to know what you wanted. And I did. You said you wanted me." He gestured sharply toward the duffel bag. "Well, this is part of what I am, Mary."

Her head had begun to ache. "Trust has nothing to do with it. Of course I want you. I want you so badly it hurts." Her voice caught. "And I'm terrified at the thought of possibly losing you."

His jaw clenched, then he said in a controlled tone, "That's not going to happen."

"It happens all the time! I know you said it was rare, but what if you were taken hostage, or—or caught in some cross fire and shot?" She moved jerkily. "I think I'd go crazy, waiting to hear whether or not you'd become 'collateral damage'. Isn't that what they call it when civilians get killed?"

He rested his hands on his hips, angling his head toward her. A lock of drying hair fell onto his brow. "I'm going to cover some meetings at the Pentagon. That's all I'm doing. You're overreacting to this."

She forced herself to breathe evenly. "I don't believe I'm overreacting."

"What exactly are you doing, then?" he demanded. "I'm packing. I've got to go. This is not a crisis. It's part of my job. I've told you not to worry, and suddenly you're panicking."

She sat down heavily on the bed and put her head in her hands. "I am trying to get you to see my point of view. You've known for a long time what you're prepared to do and been committed to doing it. But things are supposed to be different now. We're supposed to be getting married, having children, building a life together. And I need to know where the lines are."

He drew a long breath, then walked over and stroked her hair. "I do understand your point of view. It's sometimes not easy being married to someone who has to travel. But a lot of people do it. We'll work things out. I think you're going to like some of the spouses of my colleagues.''

He's not getting it, she thought bleakly. Part of him is still preoccupied with leaving and just wants to be gone. ''Will I be living the rest of my life with just half your attention? Am I going to be making coffee while you pack to leave? Can you give your dedication to me and to our children, watching them play in the backyard while you're thinking about wherever in the world you're going to be next week?''

He pulled his hand away and said tightly, ''Of course I could do both those things.''

''No, you can't! You couldn't even keep a cat. That's why you wanted to slow down, remember?''

He averted his face, nostrils flared, and muttered, ''Slow down doesn't mean stop.''

She leaned forward and said intensely, ''Please listen to me. I had good reasons for doing my job. But I still paid attention when you said it wasn't good for me! And I'm telling you your job isn't good for you, and it wouldn't be good for us.''

He looked at her and said bitterly, ''You sound so sure of that, so soon.''

''Chance, I'm not cut out to be a doctor, and I fell in love with a teacher.''

''A teacher who is a reporter, Mary!''

She looked at him pleadingly. ''I fell in love with you—your gentleness, your compassion and understanding. But when I brought your coffee in just a few minutes ago, I didn't recognize the man I was looking at.''

There was pain and anger in equal measure in his eyes. ''Is that right? Well, guess what—this is me. Maybe you fell in love with your own creation.''

She shook her head urgently. "No! I can't believe that."

"Can't you? So what are you saying, then—you don't like certain parts of me, so you won't accept them? That isn't what you promised last night," he said savagely. He jerked toward his duffel bag and yanked it shut. "I don't have time for this. Get dressed—I'm taking you home."

She said disbelievingly, "You can't leave like this—"

"The hell I can't," he snapped. "It's been an interesting week, Mary, but I've really got to go."

Her limbs had begun to grow numb. He was going. With all the hurt and misunderstandings between them, how could he still be going? She heard herself say, "If you can walk away from me right now, you really aren't who I thought you were. Don't bother coming back."

He stopped. His face, his rigid stance, everything about him went icy. "Now somehow that doesn't surprise me," he snarled. "I won't be manipulated like that. On second thought, you can find your own ride home, can't you, sweetheart? I'm sure you've got cab fare. Lock the door on your way out." He swiped the bag off the bed and strode to the door. "I'm running late."

Mary bent at the waist and put her forehead to her knees, huddling into a tight ball. The pain was incredible. Still she couldn't believe it.

He's at the top of the stairs. He'll turn around now.

Down the stairs—through the living room. Two tears slipped hotly down her face.

"Chance!" she cried out.

The front door opened and slammed. Not the Jeep. Won't he stop there?

Then the engine started outside, and he was gone.

CHAPTER TEN

MARY sat huddled on the bed for a long time, forehead bowed to her knees while the house settled into silence around her.

Finally she lifted her streaked face to stare around her dazedly. The large blue robe still smelled like him. He was etched into every part of the bedroom, and the sheets were tangled from their lovemaking that morning. She looked at the pillows that still bore the impression of their heads, hers so close to his as they kissed and whispered of all the things they looked forward to doing together.

She thought she was numb but she wasn't. Something was tearing inside her. Staying there without him was unbearable.

She lurched to her feet, gathered up her clothes and dressed. Such a pretty dress that she'd bought just for last night.

You should wear red more often, he said.

She knew she would never wear it again.

Maybe she had overreacted. Maybe she had panicked and gone too far. She'd pushed him too hard. She'd demanded things he wasn't prepared to give. He'd been thinking of the professors' families, and she had only made it worse. She had to explain things to him. They couldn't just end. How could she live without him when he had her soul? Half of him was better than nothing. If she had nothing, she was dead.

She ran downstairs, looked up the information number for the airport and dialed. When the airport switchboard answered, she was put on hold. As she waited, her feverish urgency trickled away.

He left. He left her because he wanted to leave her. He didn't say, we'll talk soon. He didn't say, I love you and I will think about what you said. All she had asked was for him not to leave her like that, and he did.

"Hello, may I help you?"

She jumped; she'd forgotten she was on hold. "I'm sorry," she whispered. "I've made a mistake." She hung up, then dialed again. It was time to go home.

She asked her grandfather to come pick her up, and he promised to be there in fifteen minutes. Then she left the diamond ring on the counter, turned off the coffeemaker and washed the carafe. She was waiting on the front porch step when her grandfather arrived.

Wallis stepped out of the station wagon, took one look at her lifeless face and blank eyes, and folded her into his arms. "What happened, kiddo?" he asked gently.

Her face screwed up. Suddenly she was sobbing against his chest, while he patted her back helplessly and told her a great many things, none of which she remembered. He bustled her into the car and they drove away.

Halfway home, she swiped her eyes and said, "I'm better now."

He nodded, scowling at the road. "I know you are."

"This isn't going to matter a year from now, is it?" she sniffed.

He shook his head, mouth compressed. "Nope."

Tears continued to sneak down her face. She caught them before they slid too far down her cheeks, peeking sideways at him. "Why—a year from now, I'll say, 'What an interesting w-w-week I had'," she wobbled. "Don't you figure?"

"I figure." They pulled to a stop, and he glared up at the stoplight, jaw working. He covered her hand with one of his. "You want to talk about it, punkin?"

She stroked his gnarled knuckles lovingly. And what would she say? Grampa, I might be pregnant. Grampa, I can't live without him. For all his ferocious bluster, he really was just a frail old man. She couldn't do that to him. "There's nothing to talk about," she said quietly. "We thought we were suited, and we aren't. I think—I think we both just wanted it so badly, you know?"

"And don't you want it anymore?"

The pain welled up again in her throat, burning hot. She forced it back and said, "I do. But I don't think he does."

He squeezed her hand hard. Then the light changed and the station wagon started to move again. Wallis cleared his throat and said, "I think you should call in sick and not go to work tonight."

She sighed and started the pretense of putting it behind her. Sooner or later she would find that she had stopped acting and it was true. People did that. They survived love affairs, broken marriages, and got on with their lives. She just had to figure out how to do that. "No, I can't do that. I just called in sick last week. Besides, it'll be better to have something to do."

Soon she would have all the time in the world on her hands, to think about all the things she wanted to do. Now it seemed to stretch endlessly in front of her. She winced away from the thought. She'd find a way to deal with that when it came. Maybe—maybe she was pregnant. A ferocious hunger gripped her. She was appalled at how much she wanted it.

Then a really sneaky part of her whispered, maybe he would want to know if you're pregnant. Maybe he would want to see the baby sometimes. You could talk together on the phone. He might come and visit.

She banged her head back on the headrest in frustration. Stop it, you're pathetic, shut up!

Wallis stared at her in alarm.

"Nothing," she mumbled. "I'm better now."

They arrived home, and she went up to her room to change out of the red dress into shorts and a T-shirt, and to wash her face. She took the outfit back downstairs and stuffed it into the trash. Janice was busy cooking lunch, and watched her with raised eyebrows.

"Don't ask," she gritted.

"I wasn't saying anything," the housekeeper said quickly.

Tim discovered she was home and came to buzz around her. She dealt with him somehow. Words happened, and he seemed satisfied with them. Eventually he buzzed away.

Then it was time for work. She dressed comfortably in light blue cotton trousers and blouse and left. More words happened as the nurses on duty greeted her cheerfully. Victor happened, with gilded malice, until she snarled quietly at him and he suddenly decided to keep well away from her.

It was a relief for once to sink into other people's problems. She was able to switch herself off, to become someone else for a time, someone who was calm and concerned and capable. Someone who knew how to fix the problems she faced.

The night passed and then it was time to go home. Life was so much easier on a schedule. She collected her purse, went outside into the bright early-morning sunshine, and sagged.

She blinked around in confusion. She couldn't remember where she'd parked. It was such a pretty day and all those damn birds were singing, and she had never felt so bereft and woebegone in all her life.

There was her car, parked right beside a black Jeep Cherokee.

That's a coincidence, she said to herself. Somebody's got a Jeep that looks just like Chance's. Any number of people have Jeep Cherokees.

Her feet seemed to be glued to the pavement, however. She stared down at them, distressed.

She seemed to be positioned so that she could see the Jeep out of one corner of her eye. As she watched her feet, the driver's door opened and somebody got out, unfolding a long, powerful, heartbreakingly familiar body.

Her head jerked up. Chance straightened, running both hands through his hair. The sunlight glinted off burnished gold. He was dressed in jeans, a black T-shirt and running shoes. From that distance he appeared to be frowning, the hard, chiseled angles of his face stark.

Incredulity, pain, gladness all surged up inside her. And no little fear. She started to shake as he strolled toward her. Why is he here? she thought. What more can he say after all the painful things we said to each other—more accusations? I'm so tired. I'm not ready for this.

She looked over her shoulder at the hospital. She looked at her car. She looked at Chance as he came to stand in front of her. There were dark shadows under his glimmering eyes.

"What a busy night I had," she said stupidly. Her heart was hammering away like a jackrabbit running for its life.

He hesitated and, for the first time since she'd known him, appeared to be at a loss. Then, gently, he said, "You must be tired. Can I drive you home?"

The gentleness hit her harder than anything else would have. She closed her eyes tight, feeling the hot tears prick again, and just shook her head.

"Mary, please," he whispered. "I have so many things to say to you."

Her voice quavered badly. "I don't want to fight again."

"I love you. I don't want to fight again, either," he said huskily. "I'm sorry, precious."

That did it. She broke, sobbed aloud, and ran toward him blindly. Strong, hard arms snatched at her; he hauled her against him, and she burrowed hungrily into his chest. He shuddered, gripping her tightly, bowing his head and shoulders around her.

"I love you," she wailed. Words tumbled out of her in a mad, uncontrolled rush. "I love you—I'm sorry for everything—I'm sorry I hung up on the airport, but you just left, you see—I thought you n-n-never wanted to talk to me again and th-th-the operator said hello—and I really couldn't th-th-think of anything to say to that—"

He exhaled sharply, face in her hair. "Mary. Sweetheart. You don't have anything to be sorry about. I shouldn't have walked out like that. You just—you just scared the hell out of me.''

She couldn't get close enough. She wanted to crawl inside his skin and live there. Her tears soaked into his T-shirt as she whispered, "I'll do anything. I'll learn how to be your wife, and—and I won't ask any questions, and I'll be right there waiting for you when you get back. I promise—I promise.''

He groaned, compulsively passing an unsteady hand over her hair. "Hush now. Mary, stop promising me things. I'm not going anywhere. I quit.''

She lifted her streaked face. "What?''

He cupped her chin. The icy stranger was gone. His face was stripped of barriers, vivid with passion and need. "I said I quit. I had time to cool down during the drive to the airport, and I thought about the things you said. Everything you said was true, precious. When I got that phone call yesterday, I stopped being me—the man I was coming to know and like, the man I wanted to be.''

She went light-headed from relief and a fierce burst of joy, but she put it aside, for the pain was back in his voice. She stroked his cheek, murmuring, "It's all right. You don't have to explain. I understand, Chance. You were dedicated for so many years—you couldn't just set it aside.''

"No, I need to say this, Mary," he said, rubbing his cheek against hers. He continued in a low voice, "That car ride to the airport was the longest journey I've ever taken. When I got there, I seemed to be seeing everything through your eyes. I couldn't understand what I was doing there. I couldn't remember why it mattered so much. All I could think about was how you looked when I left and how shattered I felt when you said you were having second thoughts about having a baby.''

She wrapped her arms around his neck, cradling his head. ''It wasn't fair to put so much pressure on you. You had so much on your mind. I knew that afterward.''

''But you were right. I even got to thinking about your being pregnant, and how I'd feel if I were half a world away. I couldn't handle it if you were having the baby without me. I need to be there, to be both a partner and a father. I can't be dedicated to both you and the job, not in the ways that I need to be.'' He sighed and nuzzled her neck. ''I just can't leave you alone. Not in any way since the first time I saw you. There wasn't any other real choice. I turned around and came home.''

She tilted her head back, closing her eyes against the brightness of the sun, while the feel of his mouth against her skin made her fingers curl with pleasure. She said dreamily, ''You stole my soul the first time you kissed me. I thought you had lots of pickle jars.''

He pulled back and stared at her. ''What?'' She explained, and he started to laugh. Rocking her gently, he crooned, ''What a lot of courage it took for you to even agree to see me at all.''

''Yes,'' she said seriously, ''I was brave. I don't think you know how terrifying you can be, Chance.''

He smoothed her hair back, framing her face with his hands, eyes dancing. ''I don't think you know how terrifying *you* can be.''

Her eyes went very wide and her mouth dropped open. ''Me?''

''Yes, you.'' He chuckled. ''You look so surprised. From the first time you told me to get out of the way,

I was hooked. I kept coming back. You were such a puzzle, I couldn't figure you out. There was no telling what was going to make you squeak and run, or what might make you reach out to me with open arms. I decided I had to kiss this delightful little enigma I had taken home just to see what it would do, and then I found us both going up in flames. God, you shook me."

She smiled. "Were we doomed?"

"I think so." His gaze dropped to her lips, and he grew serious. He bent and covered her mouth so reverently, she whimpered and held on to him tightly. He drew back and whispered, "You're the best teacher I've ever had."

"I know you're mine," she said softly, glowing up at him. "Think of everything we've got to learn together."

Her red-rimmed eyes were luminous. A light breeze lifted wavy strands of her hair and blew them around her face like dandelion fluff. She was so unaware of the gentle power she had, but her transparent joy tugged at him constantly, like the moon's command over the ocean. His entire world was encapsulated in that small, emphatic package. He would spend his life protecting and cherishing her.

The jewel-like gleam of her blue eyes reminded him. He reached into his pocket and drew out her engagement ring, still remembering what a blow it had been to find it on his kitchen counter. He stared down at it, and his throat muscles worked. "This is yours," he said hoarsely, fumbling for her left hand to put the ring where it belonged. "Don't ever take it off again."

She heard past the imperative demand in his voice to the need that impelled him, and she closed her hand around the ring. "I never will," she said quietly. "You're home, and I am yours."

He looked at her searchingly. Then he closed his eyes and such a look of peace came over his face, she nearly cried again. He drew a breath and said, "Come on, sugar. Let's go."

He slipped an arm around her waist and walked with her to the cars. She rested her head against his shoulder and said happily, "What a fine morning it is."

He smiled. "Isn't it," he agreed.

She nestled against him. "Chance, I don't want to drive."

"You're not going to." He led her to the passenger side of the Jeep, opened the door and lifted her in. Then he followed, pressing her back against the seat as he kissed her hard. She moaned, her lips parting and he plunged into the delicate, moist crevice of her mouth, ravenously drinking from her.

She twisted under his heavy weight, straining to get closer as she sank her hands into the hair at the back of his head. Then she shivered and clung to him, because the incredulity had not quite left her after so much pain, and he pulled back to enfold her tenderly.

"I want to do everything we planned to do yesterday," he said gruffly. "But you need breakfast and bed. Are you up to facing your grandfather and Tim?"

She nodded. Poor Grampa, he deserves to hear how things worked out after I worried him so badly yesterday. "I want to." Then her forehead wrinkled as she plucked at his shirt. "Did you sleep much last night?"

"No," he murmured.

She put her face in his neck and inhaled his scent. "Are you very tired, too?"

His voice roughened. "Most definitely too tired to do anything without you." He caressed her slender thighs.

She leaned her hot forehead against his collarbone. His pulse had accelerated, and he was breathing deeply. "What are we going to say to them?" she sighed, so hungry for him she couldn't think straight.

"We'll tell them we're engaged, you'll go to your room to pack an overnight bag, and we'll go back to my place. Quickly," he added with a tight grin.

The predator was back, sleek and poised to pounce. It looked at her from the richness of his unblinking eyes and said, Soon.

But he, too, had been hurt recently, and there was a lingering hint of question.

Soon, she promised, and for the first time she welcomed the predator, unafraid. He saw how wholeheartedly she meant it, and the question faded, leaving him exultant.

The trip home was a heated prelude. Chance took her hand as they walked toward the house, and she clasped it between both of hers. She couldn't stop touching him, and she stroked his long fingers, remembering the intensity of the pleasure he'd given her. She could tell by the darkened flush along his cheekbones and the glitter in his eyes that he was remembering, too.

She took a long breath. First things first. Letting go of his hand, she danced up the porch steps while he purred up behind her. She opened the front door and sang out, "Hi, everybody, I'm home!"

There was one moment when the scene of the front hall and staircase was serenely quiet. Then it seemed the whole world descended on them.

Wallis yanked open the study door, caught sight of Chance, and his face purpled. Cassie shot out of the library, Tim on her heels.

Cassie?

Mary stopped dead and Chance bumped into her. His hands went around her waist quickly to keep her from falling.

Wallis strode toward them, bellowing, "You have a hell of a lot of nerve coming here after treating my baby girl like that!"

"Sir," Chance said firmly.

Cassie was dressed in a gray sweat suit, red hair back in a ponytail. Her eyes were blazing. She stalked down the hall, one fist clenched, and hissed, "This time I'm really gonna kill you, Chance."

Mary ogled her in shock, shrinking back instinctively. Chance's arms came around her, and he said soothingly in her ear, "It's all right. Everything's under control."

Wallis was still shouting. Cassie looked at her, and her face softened. "Hi, Mary," she crooned gently. "Would you get out of my way, please?"

Mary pushed back against Chance harder and shook her head. He was starting to shake with laughter.

Tim's head popped up from behind Cassie's shoulder, eyes shining with excitement, and he waved. "You were having such a bad day yesterday, so I naturally thought of calling Cassie to see if we could help.

She came over right away," he said in an awed voice. "Hi, Mary. Hi, Chance."

"Hi, Tim," Chance said cheerfully.

"Er—just a minute," said Mary.

". . . and I'll give you one final chance to unhand my granddaughter!" Wallis cried.

". . . just answer me this, you big idiot!" Cassie snarled. "Why the *hell* did you drag me all over town to buy the love of your life a ring if you were gonna walk out on her the next day!"

"Excuse me, everybody," Mary said.

"I want an explanation, and I want it now!" Wallis yelled.

Mary felt Chance inhale deeply, and his body stiffened. "QUIET!" he roared over her head. The deep, powerful shout echoed off the walls like a gunshot.

Silence. Wallis and Cassie stared at him with deep offense, while Tim, big-eyed, stood very straight.

Chance said more quietly, "Mary and I had a bad time. It's over now. I'm retiring, and we're getting married in a week and a half."

They all looked at her. She held up her left hand, waggled her engagement ring at them and beamed.

After a long pause, Wallis said, "Oh."

The storm clouds left Cassie's face and she threw her arms around them both in an exuberant embrace. "Yes! I knew you wouldn't be that stupid," she assured her brother. "But what're you going to do with yourself now?"

He shrugged. "Schubert offered me a permanent position at the university, which I may end up taking after Mary and I talk about it. I've got options. We'll see."

Tim was hanging back quietly. Mashed as she was between Chance and Cassie, Mary didn't see him, but Chance did. Keeping one arm around Mary, he held out the other to her brother. "Congratulate us, son?"

Mary put an arm around Cassie's neck as she turned to look. She saw Tim's face, vulnerable and looking very young, and Chance's warm, reassuring smile. Then Tim shot across the hall and was pulled into the general huddle. "I'm glad," he whispered to Mary.

"Me, too," she whispered back and kissed him.

Wallis crossed his arms and glared at the four. "I guess I'd better go open a bottle of champagne or something," he growled, and he turned to stump toward the kitchen.

Cassie laughed out loud. "Come on, Tim," she said. "Let's leave these lovebirds and go help Grampa."

"Okay," he sighed, and he trailed away behind her.

Chance turned Mary around to face him, remnants of laughter still in his eyes. He looked young, carefree. As she spread her hands across his chest, he bent down to kiss her deeply. Passion curled tight inside her, and she leaned against him with a shaken groan.

"I love you," he said fiercely.

Her heart leapt. "I love you," she whispered in reply. "We aren't going to get away as quickly as we hoped, are we?"

"No." He lifted her hair away from the nape of her neck and cradled her head. "But it doesn't matter, precious. Now we have all the time in the world."

He was right, they did.

She rested against him and was content.

CHAPTER ELEVEN

"REALLY?" Mary cried.

"Yes, really," Julie, the nurse from the hospital, assured her. "Congratulations. And oh, by the way— congratulations, too, on getting married last weekend. We put the notice up in the doctors' lounge. You should have seen Victor's face. It would have curdled milk."

"Oh, him!" she exclaimed dismissively. Victor was nothing more to her than a distant splotch on her past horizon. "Thank you so much for everything, Julie."

"Honestly, it was my pleasure. We miss you, and we miss your hunky hubby picking you up every day. All the other nurses have quite a crush on him. I don't, of course."

Mary laughed delightedly, promised to meet Julie for lunch the next week, said goodbye and hung up. Then she hugged herself, looking around their bedroom. Chance had liked the peach-and-green color scheme, and the room had been spacious enough to move in his dressers and one of his bookshelves.

She had to find him. She straightened her rose-patterned skirt in the full-length mirror and waltzed down the stairs toward the back door. The smells of the Sunday dinner made her pause, and humming, she went to check on the large capon roasting in the oven. It was nearly ready. She tucked the foil-wrapped potatoes to one side and put the tray of crescent rolls in to bake.

Outside she went. Cassie and her father, Johnny, were playing a cutthroat game of croquet on the lawn in the same spot where the wedding had been held a week ago. In a nearby pavilion, Carmen and Wallis stretched out in lounge chairs, drinking wine and talking as they watched the game.

They waved at her, and she waved back as she hurried to the large shed where Chance and Tim were plotting on how to fix the damaged yacht Chance had bought from Harold Schubert. She didn't quite understand yet how they were going to go about repairing the *Gypsy Dancer*. It seemed to involve bottles of beer and cans of soda, and many hours of talking in the shed. She suspected it might involve the professional help of a shipyard before it was over, but both Chance and Tim were enjoying themselves so much, she kept her mouth shut.

She waltzed up to the open doors and peered inside.

The thirty-foot yacht, cradled on the boat trailer, dominated the middle space of the shed. Chance, clad in a white shirt and tan trousers, was bent over a workbench against one wall, studying designs, while Tim hovered at his elbow. As if aware of her presence by some sixth sense, Chance looked up.

She never failed to be amazed at how he lit up when he saw her. He pushed away from the bench to stroll toward her, raking his hair back with one hand, while her gaze ran possessively down the length of his body, and she thought, You're mine, you beautiful man.

He stepped out into the sunshine. "Hello, sweetheart, is dinner ready? What can I do to help?"

She clasped her hands together. "Chance, I'm pregnant."

He froze, staring at her incredulously. She nodded at him, beaming. Then his face ignited with joy, and with a war whoop he darted forward to swing her up. She threw her arms around his neck, laughing tearfully as he twirled her around.

"When did you find out?" he demanded.

"Just now, on the phone. Remember when I had to run errands this morning? I stopped at the hospital, and Julie had one of the technicians run a test just for me."

"My God, you kept a secret!"

She lifted one shoulder, looking proud. "Well, for a couple of hours."

He stopped and dipped his head for a long, deep kiss. She nuzzled against him, purring. "You precious, precious thing," he whispered. "You're my universe."

Mary looked serenely up at the sky. She knew she was. He proved it in many ways every day. "You're mine, too."

"Oh, my God," Tim said from behind them, "I'm going to be an uncle!"

They turned to look. His eyes were bugged out. Mary started to laugh again helplessly. "Don't look so scared, honey. It'll be all right."

"I'm going to be a father," Chance breathed. "I'm looking forward to every terrifying minute of it. Let's go tell everybody now."

Mary nodded and looked at the ground, expecting to be put down, but he held on to her tight. While Tim ran ahead, Chance stepped lightly around the corner of the shed and followed with a lilting step, dancing with her in his arms.

BRIDE'S BAY RESORT

UNLOCK THE DOOR TO GREAT ROMANCE AT BRIDE'S BAY RESORT

Join Harlequin's new across-the-lines series, set in an exclusive hotel on an island off the coast of South Carolina.

Seven of your favorite authors will bring you exciting stories about fascinating heroes and heroines discovering love at Bride's Bay Resort.

Look for these fabulous stories coming to a store near you beginning in January 1996.

Harlequin American Romance #613 in January
Matchmaking Baby by Cathy Gillen Thacker

Harlequin Presents #1794 in February
Indiscretions by Robyn Donald

Harlequin Intrigue #362 in March
Love and Lies by Dawn Stewardson

Harlequin Romance #3404 in April
Make Believe Engagement by Day Leclaire

Harlequin Temptation #588 in May
Stranger in the Night by Roseanne Williams

Harlequin Superromance #695 in June
Married to a Stranger by Connie Bennett

Harlequin Historicals #324 in July
Dulcie's Gift by Ruth Langan

Visit Bride's Bay Resort each month wherever Harlequin books are sold.

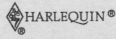

HARLEQUIN ®

BBAYG

HARLEQUIN  PRESENTS®

PRIVATE & CONFIDENTIAL

MEMO

To: The Reader

From: The Editor at Harlequin Presents

Subject: #1829 BEYOND ALL REASON
by Cathy Williams

Abigail knew her gorgeous boss, Ross Anderson, couldn't seriously be attracted to her. But should Abigail listen to reason, or follow her heart?

P.S. Available in August wherever Harlequin books are sold.

NINE2

HARLEQUIN PRESENTS®

Just a taste!

Sample the exciting new story from top author
Jacqueline Baird:

#1827 *A Devious Desire*

"Wait, Alex.... Marriage is a big step—are you sure
you're ready for it? You have been a bachelor for an
awful long time."

"Marriage? Who mentioned marriage?" He let go of
her and stepped back as if he had been stung.

"I'm sorry if I misunderstood," she said softly, acting for
all she was worth. "But I'm afraid that's the only way
you'll ever get me."

Will Saffron snare Alex and get her revenge?

Available in August wherever Harlequin books are sold.

TAUTH-11

You are cordially invited to a

HOMETOWN REUNION

September 1996—August 1997

Where can you find romance and adventure,
bad boys, cowboys, feuding families, and babies,
arson, mistaken identity, a mom on the run...?
Tyler, Wisconsin, that's where!

So join us in this not-so-sleepy little town and
experience the love, the laughter and the
tears of those who call it home.

WELCOME TO A
HOMETOWN REUNION

Twelve unforgettable stories, written for you by
some of Harlequin's finest authors. This fall,
begin a yearlong affair with America's favorite
hometown as **Marisa Carroll** brings you
Unexpected Son.

Available at your favorite retail store.

◆HARLEQUIN ®
®

HTRG

Four years ago Darcy made a pass at heartthrob
Keir Robards. And he turned her down flat.

BUT

NOW

HE'S

BACK!

And Darcy is determined to make him pay....

#1831 FAST AND LOOSE
by Elizabeth Oldfield

Available in August wherever
Harlequin books are sold.

HARLEQUIN PRESENTS®

Look us up on-line at: http://www.romance.net